Tell Them
I Died

by

Sarah Gordon Weathersby

Published by Sarah Weathersby
www.sarahweathersby.com

ISBN-13: 978-0615703190

ISBN-10: 0615703194

Printed in the United States of America.

Cover design by Cynthia M. Colbert

In loving memory of

Foxy

JWBaldi

MsCreole

GMack

ACKNOWLEDGMENTS

Thank you God, for keeping me, keeping me alive and whole and writing through it all. Thank you for giving me this story. May it provide a laugh or smile, as it has for me through times of trial. Thank you to my Sweetie, my "Verbal Mind Keeper."

My love and gratitude to my early readers, Sherry McFarland, the Mahogany Experience writing group, Facebook friends and Urbandour Alumni. Thank you to Erin Morgenstern, whom I have never met, but whose pep talk to Nanowrimo 2011 propelled my head out of a three-year Nano-block, and lifted my fingers across the keys to the finish. Thank you for the "wise and ancient NaNo wisdom: when in doubt, just add ninjas." Thank you Linda Dorsey, who introduced me to the services provided to American Express Gold Card holders, especially useful for a stranded traveler. Thank you Cynthia Marie, I can't imagine a book with my name, and not have your artwork on the cover. You took my goofy idea and turned it into a cover that pops. I have come to trust your artistic judgement.

And to my editor, Shonell Bacon (http://shonellbacon.com), thank you for your gentle insistence to cut the backstory, forget the Karma. And for all the times you told me, "Make me see it." The journey was so much sweeter with you to guide and teach me.

And to you, dear readers, thank you for taking this ride with me.

CHAPTER ONE

Screen Name: A1QTEE - Sunday Night

Finally found the missing eighteen dollars, Angela said to herself as she balanced her checkbook in her Money program. I can go to bed now. When she heard her cell phone playing *Heard it Through the Grapevine*, she saw on the Caller ID it was QTEE. *Haven't heard from you in over a month. Can't you remember we're three hours later here in Raleigh than you are in Vegas?* She clicked the phone on and said, "Hello Laura," expecting her friend's usual "Hello Beautiful," but a male voice responded.

"Ms. Angela, this is Carlton, Laura's son. She would have wanted me to tell you. She died last month."

Angela gasped. "NO. What happened?"

"You probably know she had heart trouble. I went to check on her that day, and she had died in her sleep." Carlton's voice was without emotion. Different people have their own way of grieving, she thought.

"I'm so sorry, Carlton. You know she meant a lot to me. So the funeral, everything is over then?" Angela got up from her chair and paced the room trying to keep from crying. She felt the pain rising up in her chest and the tears welling up in her eyes.

"It was just me and Mom, you know. She hadn't talked to her family in New York for a long time. She didn't want a funeral, just a cremation."

Angela needed to find some way of holding onto the memory of her internet friend. "Was there a program or obituary...anything?"

"No ma'am. We had a viewing at the funeral home, but nobody came."

Angela had never met Carlton or talked to him before, but she knew he was his mother's heart. Only three months earlier when QTEE was going to marry Jackson and move to Memphis, she had transferred the title of her condo to Carlton. Laura had made sure he would not have to want for anything if he managed his finances.

"Are you doing OK? She told me you had gotten married. She posted pictures of the baby all over the site." Angela was starting to ramble. She didn't know what to say. "Is there anything you need? Do you need help getting things in order?"

"I think I need to talk to a lawyer to help me handle the will and Mom's expenses," Carlton replied, his voice whining, "and I don't know how I'm going to pay for it. Maybe you could tell the others on the site we...I could use a donation to get Mom's business straight."

Angela stopped pacing and stared out the window into the

darkness of the woods. QTEE had been open about having enough money, between her Army pension, and alimony, so she didn't need to work. Why was he asking for money?

Carlton went on. "Do you think I should call Jackson? Mom had his number in her cell phone even though she didn't talk to him after they broke up, and she changed all her phone numbers."

"I think he would want to know," Angela replied. "He should hear it from you."

"OK, I'll call him."

"Why don't you wait until morning? It's already close to eleven here. I'll give him a call too tomorrow."

Angela thanked him for letting her know, and said she would be in touch.

The tears started to flow. She had seen Laura only twice in the flesh, but they had been friends online for over five years. Laura was "A1QTEE" on the social networking site Blaq-kawfee.com where she was owner-operator. Angela was "Angelplaits" and a moderator on the site, not to mention Laura's number one confidante. Laura and Jackson had had a long-distance relationship for as long as Angela had known them. He flew to Las Vegas to see her only months ago, asked Carlton for his permission to marry his Mom, and gave her a ring. Then it all started to unravel.

Angela shut off her computer and cried again before looking around the mess on her desk and deciding to leave it as it was. Yellow post-it notes framed her PC monitor with names and phone numbers she might need in the coming week. Appointment cards from the dentist, radiologist, gynecologist, massage therapist obscured the photos of her grandsons stuck in the corners of her desk blotter. And there was the pile of debit card receipts she hadn't gotten around to entering into her Money program. Her husband Bodine's desk on the other side of their home office was neat. He had shut off his machine over an hour ago.

He had left a dim lamp on for her in their bedroom, where he had turned down the comforter and stacked the matching pillows on top of the bed bench. She heard him snoring softly as she climbed into bed beside him. Many nights he went to bed before she did. He was active online; they had met on Match.com and married five years ago. He knew about Laura and Jackson's rocky romance, but was never as pulled into it as Angela was. She wanted to wake him to tell him, but she could tell by the way his closed eyes moved, he wouldn't remember anything she might say that night.

After tossing and turning for over an hour, she decided to slip back into their office and call Jackson. It would be an hour earlier in Memphis.

"JackDaniels, it's me Angelplaits."

"Angela, to what do I owe this honor?" She could hear the smile in his voice.

"It's awful, Jackson." How should she say this? Best to spit it out. "Laura is dead."

He gasped, "What?"

"Carlton called me tonight. I was going to wait until the

morning to tell you, but I couldn't sleep. She died a month ago."

Jackson's heavy breathing was all Angela heard on the other end, until he said, "Nooooo. How did it happen?"

Jackson was a dear man. They cried together on the phone, both of them heartbroken over the loss, and hurt at not knowing sooner. He told Angela his side of the break-up with Laura. She had been stubborn. Didn't consider his feelings. He wanted to make up with her, but she had cut him off. He laughed about how many times she had changed her phone numbers. Landline, cell phone, and she had a "business number" she used when dealing with the site-hosting company and her technical support. He admitted he never took her business as seriously as she did.

Jackson couldn't hold it back, "Damn expensive hobby. Blaq-Kawfee was costing her $500 a month. And she didn't allow advertising. She had to run the Rooibos tea guy off the site when y'all didn't like what he was selling."

"I told Carlton he should call you in the morning." Angela didn't know what else to say.

Jackson continued, "That boy is too young to handle Laura's business. He's only twenty-one. I know she left the condo to him. She signed it over to him when we were going to get married. That and everything else she had."

"I know he's young, but it bothered me when he asked if I could get the friends on the site to make a donation to him," Angela confided.

Jackson's sorrow turned to anger. "Donation? What for? He

took care of the cremation, didn't he, without calling anybody. I don't understand why he decided to call after a month. That's not right. It's just not right. Look, Angela, I'm not going to sleep tonight. I have to think this thing through. I'll call you in the morning. Something doesn't feel right about this."

Angela tried to soothe him. "I know this thing hit you out of the blue. I'm upset, too. Do you think it would help if we had some kind of online memorial? I'm going to have to tell everybody on Blaq-Kawfee in the morning."

"You do what you want to. You say he asked for a donation like Laura did for Lil-Miss after Hurricane Katrina. That's wrong."

Angela knew he was right, but she said, "You sleep on it. We'll talk in the morning."

"We'll talk, but I won't be sleeping."

Angela settled back into her bed and tossed the whole night. Bodine got up to go to the bathroom around 3 a.m. and asked her what was bothering her to make her so agitated.

"QTEE died, honey. It happened a month ago, and her son called last night."

Bodine hugged her in one of his big bear hugs, "My little angel." Angela engulfed herself in his scent, an aromatherapy taking her dreams to home, far away from her worries about other people's business.

CHAPTER TWO

Screen Name: JackDaniels - Monday Morning

The phone rang at 6:22 a.m., shaking Angela from a deep sleep. When the talking Caller ID announced in its computer droning voice, "Call from Memphis Tenn.," Bodine rolled over. Angela jumped up to get it.

"JackDaniels? Is that you?" She was still groggy.

"Sorry to call so early, but I'm catching the first plane out to Las Vegas. I have to get some information first hand."

"But Jackson," Angela reverted to real names when conversations became serious, "Your health is not that good. Man, should you be traveling?"

"I have to do this," he said.

"What do you think you can find out in person that you can't get from a phone call?"

Jackson insisted. "I'm going to the police. I won't be hung up on. If Laura died alone, there would have to be a police report. I'll have to find the mortuary. Do you have Carlton's number?"

"Carlton called me from Laura's phone, and I didn't ask for his number," Angela said. "I had been calling the same number over the past month and it always went straight to voicemail. I think the only reason he turned it on was to get our phone numbers. I hope you can find out something. Please keep me posted. I'm worried about you traveling like this."

"I'll let you know what I find out."

Angela remembered when she first came to know Jackson on Blaq-Kawfee. He started a forum called "Jack Daniels' Place." He and some other male members liked to joke about drinking. When he posted something about needing a funnel, Angela jumped in and asked what they were talking about. Jackson thought it was hilarious that she didn't understand. He started referring to her as "The Nun...because she can't get none." For revenge, Angela posted a Photoshopped photo of herself dressed in a habit, and started a forum called "Sister Angela's Confessional." People had fun posting their confessions and Angela would respond with instructions for saying Hail Mary's and would tell them to call her in the morning. Over time, people started sending her private messages with their real problems, asking for her help. She didn't tell anybody about those requests; they were secrets she kept.

Angela was wide awake now. As two retired people, she and Bodine rarely got up before seven. After only a few hours of sleep, she wasn't rested—her mind was back on Laura. She had to tell the others on Blaq-Kawfee.

When Angela logged on, it occurred to her the site might not be around for long with nobody paying the hosting fees. They had all missed Laura from the site for the last month, but it was not unusual for her to take a long hiatus from the site after one of her break-ups with Jackson. During those spells, she would often create another ID to see what was happening and not allow anyone to see her.

Angela busied herself with finding a nice photo of Laura so she could post an entry on the site, "Remembering A1QTEE." There wasn't much she could tell people other than what Carlton had told her. It started hurting again. She told herself she had to excuse him. He's young, and he's not active online. People who didn't have internet friendships didn't get it. They didn't understand how deep those relationships could be.

There were only three people on the site at such an early time in the morning, and they responded to Angela's post with disbelief. Angela didn't tell them Jackson was on the way to Las Vegas to dig for information.

When Lester ("TheGuy") came online, he said what some others were afraid to say. "Laura's messing with us. She can't be dead. You know how she's always pulling her disappearing acts."

Angela decided she wouldn't respond, and let the others toss it around among themselves. Lester was one of Laura's favorites. He liked stirring up controversy. Many of the members admitted Lester was the main reason they liked coming online several times a day. He kept so much drama going on. He got into trouble when he violated one of Laura's rules: "No name-calling on the site." She had banished him from the site more than once. After one time he said he would not be back, but Laura missed him so much she asked Angela to find him and ask him to come back. It wasn't difficult to find Lester. There were several other social networking sites frequented by Blaq-Kawfee members. Angela found him and told him Laura missed him. They made up, and he didn't break the rules again after that. Except for the few people who were so clueless he could call them names without their understanding he was insulting them.

This was one of those rare times when Angela thought, I'll close this window, and it will all go away.

By that time Angela could smell breakfast cooking downstairs. Bodine had slipped into some jeans and was already back from taking Dusty out for a walk. Angela thought what a treasure her husband was. She had to shake her head at their pooch with his shaggy curly hair the color of a dust mop. She loved dogs, but it was Bodine's decision to get a dog although they were away every month. The poor thing would have to spend two weeks in doggy day care while they went on their next cruise. They had been lucky to find a couple who would board him at their house. Bodine had rescued his sweet dust mop from the animal shelter only two months ago.

Bodine was planning what he would do for the day. Some days he spent as much time on Blaq-Kawfee as Angela did, but on a sunny day like this one, he could be found outside. He liked having some kind of project, his garden and his fix-it and building projects around the house. Angela had her schedule of volunteer work. It was her turn to take her care partner to his dialysis appointment. They both had something to keep them busy and away from the computer.

Angela's care partner was Isaiah, a short man she referred to as "My Little Man." He was no more than 5'2" tall, weighing ninety pounds. His body was ravaged by AIDS, along with complications of kidney and heart disease. He lived with his daughter who did all she could for him, but his dialysis schedule conflicted with her work schedule. When Angela picked him up, his daughter kissed him goodbye and said, "I love you, Daddy." He said he loved her, too. He always greeted Angela with an upbeat observation of the day.

"I don't know when I have seen such a clear blue sky." And he would go on inquiring about Angela's family. Angela told him about her sons who both lived a few miles away in Durham. Isaiah inquired about her younger son, Stephen, after Angela told Isaiah about Stephen's accident and spinal cord injury years ago. "How does that young one manage, living alone?"

"His brother Aaron calls him every day, and sometimes they meet for lunch. It's important to Stephen to have his own place. He loves being independent. Ever since he was given his network engineer job with Duke University Health System, he's been managing on his own."

Isaiah settled into the back seat. Angela's team leader joked about how he would take the back seat and make her feel like Miss Daisy in reverse, driving her old gentleman. He slept most of the twenty-minute ride to Wake Med. He liked to arrive early so he could use his meal voucher and have breakfast in the cafeteria before his dialysis. Angela dropped him off at the door and continued to do her errands for the day. Another team member would pick Isaiah up and take him home.

Bodine didn't understand Angela's ministry as she called it. He didn't like to think about AIDS or people dying. He went to funerals only for immediate family. Angela, on the other hand would go visit people in the hospital and keep up with the sick and elderly she had known for years. She had been to two funerals for her AIDS care partners, and expected to attend Isaiah's funeral if he was still around when they returned from the cruise. She had told Isaiah she would see him in a month. He had said, "I might not see you, but you may see me."

Angela spent the rest of the morning running errands, and went back home to do her weekly updates on the website she managed for the church. She included the announcements from Sunday in the online calendar, as well as in the "What's Happening" section on the site's homepage.

It was late in the day before Jackson called. "Angela, I can't get anywhere. The police won't tell me anything. They claim they don't have anything about a Laura Murchison. They sent me from Homicide to the Coroner's Office and back, and they wanted to fingerprint me. I had a time getting out of there and not getting arrested."

"What about Carlton? Was he any help?" Angela asked.

"I couldn't find Carlton. Nobody was answering at the condo. I even asked the condo security about Laura's death, and they said they couldn't give out that kind of information. They took my picture, and copied my ID to put in some file." Angela could hear the frustration in Jackson's voice.

It was Angela's nature to want to help. "Somebody on Blaq-Kawfee ought to know who can help. I'll get online and ask questions. I know a couple of women on the site who live in Vegas. Besides, somebody ought to know Carlton. You get some rest, Jackson. When is your return ticket?"

"I left my return flight open. I'm determined to learn something about Laura's death."

"I'll call you back when I know more," Angela said. "Oh, yes, what about the mortuary? Did you get any info there?"

"I need to get a list of mortuaries in the area since I can't find Carlton. I'm on my way to the public library to use the free wi-fi."

"If you need me to search for anything from my end, I can do that and email you a list."

"That would be a big help. Thanks Angela."

When Angela logged back onto Blaq-Kawfee, she could see there were over twenty discussion threads about Laura's death. There were over fifty people online, more than usual for the site. Laura intentionally kept BK small and cozy. She preferred to be able to have a personal friendship with all the members than to have so many who would add to her expense for server space and traffic.

Angela browsed through the discussions and read most people were grieving and hurting the same way. Paulo from South America was also online. He didn't usually join in on the discussion threads. Angela thought it was because of the language difference, but there he was talking about Laura, and how he would miss her. The longest thread contained plans to have a memorial service online through one of the online talk radio stations. Angela made a list of who was online, and sent out an alert for people in Las Vegas, anyone who knew Carlton and how to reach him. The response was immediate. There were two women who lived in Vegas and offered their help. One had met Carlton and knew where he lived.

Angela was pondering whether to call Jackson when a call came in from Laura's phone number. It was Carlton again.

"Hi, Ms. Angela. It's me, Carlton, Laura's son again. I was looking through Mama's things from the mortuary and I found what they printed out about her death. I thought it was something you might want to have."

Thanks, I'd love to have it. Carlton, what is the name of the mortuary?"

"Oh, Ms. Angela, it's on the thing, and I put it in the mail already. It's Johnson and Blackman, or Johns and Blackston, or something like that. I can't keep names in my head. But you'll get it in a few days."

Angela said, "I realized after we talked the last time I didn't have your phone number, only this number from your mom's phone."

"I'm in the process of moving and I'm changing my numbers." Carlton said. "I'll give you a call when I get my new number."

"Thanks Carlton." Angela said, but she still didn't understand what he was up to. Why did he call if he wasn't going to tell her anything?

Now Angela was starting to shake. Like Jackson had said, it wasn't right. She had never known anyone so evasive.

She called Jackson to give him the contacts from Blaq-Kawfee.

"Bonita and Stacey live in Las Vegas, and want to help. Bonita knows that guy Robbie who tried to sell Rooibos tea on Blaq-Kawfee. He lives somewhere near Laura's condo. Bonita thinks he might want to help."

She told him about the conversation with Carlton.

Jackson said, "See. I told you it wasn't right. I don't know what to make of it. I don't want to go accusing that boy of doing something awful, but he sure is covering something up. I'll look into those Johns and Blackman or whatever names and see if there is a mortuary with a similar name. I kind of doubt it. I'm thinking if I can get to the 911 operators from the day she died, I could get some useful information. They have to record every call."

Angela was always the worrywart. "I'm not feeling good about your being out there snooping around where nobody knows you. Call those girls and see if they will help...at least have somebody who knows what you might be getting into."

"OK, I'll call them." Jackson said. "And the one with the tea, I don't know about him. Remember he got nasty when y'all asked about where he bought the tea he was selling. He started the name-calling until Laura had to banish him from the site. She told me he started harassing her with phone calls after that. I'd better tell Bonita and Stacey to back off from him."

"Were you able to get any rest this afternoon?"

"Nah, Angela. I don't think I will until I get some answers."

"I told you, I'm worried about you."

"I'll be fine," Jackson reassured her. "Don't worry."

Angela went back to her PC and joined the discussion about a memorial. Several members had already collaborated on a beautiful graphic with Laura at the center with all the friends around her. The poets in the group had added some original poems for the memorial. Some of the members in the Washington DC area thought it would be good to have a real service at one of the DC area churches since they made up the largest group from one place. Dillon agreed it would be easy to do since he already had the Meet & Greet membership list. People who were not active on Blaq-Kawfee who knew Laura from other websites would want to come as well. Dillon said he would inquire at his church about having the service there.

Angela checked one of the other discussion threads. There were several people who still doubted if Laura was dead. "Wouldn't we look like a fool if she showed up at her own memorial?" Angela was having doubts herself. The memorials on the site were good, but she would have to tell Dillon what was happening with Jackson in Las Vegas.

She sent Dillon a private message:

Dillon,

Please hold off on doing anything with a public memorial service for Laura. JackDaniels is in Las Vegas trying to get the details on Laura's death. He's not having much luck finding Laura's son Carlton. We have some members on the site who live in Vegas and have agreed to help track him down.

Thanks,

Angela

Angela didn't want to tell too much about Jackson's meeting with the police. She didn't want to feed the detractors. She didn't want to believe Carlton had lied. Why would he lie about his mother's death? Nobody had heard anything from Laura in over a month. Why did Carlton call now? Whatever the truth was, Carlton knew.

When Angela told Bodine what had happened, he wanted her to back off from the whole thing.

"Why is this your problem? If she's dead, she's dead and the funeral or whatever is over. If JackDaniels wants to be out there looking, that's on him. You're getting too worked up over this," he said.

"But Honey, what if Laura is alive?"

"If she's alive and safe, she's trying to make a fool of all of us, and we need to move on. If she's not safe, then Carlton is lying." Bodine had his way of simplifying any problem.

"What if she didn't die naturally? What if somebody killed her?" Angela asked. In her mind, there was always something to worry about.

"Who would want to kill QTEE? What motive would they have? Wouldn't the police know if there was a murder?"

One thing Angela had admired about Bodine from the beginning of their relationship was his way of separating himself from anything that might drag him down. He wasn't going to worry himself about Laura. Angela, on the other hand, was the ultimate worrywart. Bodine called her "Chuckie," after the kid in the Rugrats cartoon show because she would always say, "I don't know...something might happen."

She tossed and turned another night until the talking Caller ID voice announced, "Call from Las Vegas, NV." It annoyed Angela how the voice tried to pronounce NV, as a word and not as separate letters. She reached for the phone, not looking at the clock. Her eyes couldn't focus on it anyway in the dark without her glasses. She knew it was Jackson.

"Why did you set me up like that?" he asked.

"What? Jackson? What happened?

"Those two women, Bonita and Stacey. They were expecting a Good Time Charlie or something. I told them I needed to talk to the police and the mortuary. They took me on a tour of the Strip, pointing out all the casinos, telling me about the free things to see.

They insisted on parking the car at Bellagio so we could go look at the fountains. When we went downtown, I thought we were going to the police, but we wound up on Freemont Street, watching the light show. I was so tired I was ready to go back to my hotel. But then they said they would take me to see Carlton. They said they knew where he lived."

"Did you see him?" Angela asked.

"First they had to stop at Bonita's house. Bonita had dinner ready and all, so I ate. Both of those women turned out to be freaks. They changed into lingerie and tried to seduce me. Finally I hollered. Just give me the boy's address, and let me out of here."

Angela could hear his frustration, but she had to ask, "Did you get the address?"

"I got the address." Jackson said. "But first they had to call me some kind of low-life snake to take up their time and eat their food and on and on. I almost cried, please, please. They let me call a taxi, and I went out and sat on Bonita's front steps to wait."

"I'm sorry. I had no idea. I only know those women from Blaq-Kawfee. I guess I should have known since Laura didn't associate with them. I don't even know what time it is. I suppose it was too late after all your running around for you to find Carlton."

Jackson said, "I know I said I wouldn't rest until I found Laura, but after tonight I need to get some sleep. I'll track down Carlton tomorrow."

CHAPTER THREE

Tuesday

Jackson hardly knew what day it was. He had been awake over twenty-four hours, and although he was tired, he knew he still would not sleep soundly. He showered and dressed so he would be ready for his morning trip to find Carlton. He set the clock for six a.m. and lay down on the bed fully clothed. At least he'd had a good meal at Bonita's house. Now he could laugh at how ridiculous that scene had been.

Internet hoochie-mamas. Those girls were so tame online. I never would have guessed. And Stacey was married. Laura probably had them all figured out, but Angela was so naïve. What a set-up.

He slept for a few hours before the alarm rang. This time he drove his rental car and picked up a cup of black coffee on his way. The built-in GPS took him to Carlton's place in a short time. Carlton lived in a small bungalow on a quiet street. Jackson parked down the block where he could see Carlton whenever he left. After Angela told him how he lied, he didn't want to take a chance on being dodged.

The front door opened after Jackson had been waiting close to an hour. A young woman with a toddler emerged. Jackson recognized them as Carlton's wife and baby. He had never met them, but had seen photos Laura had posted on the web. Jackson headed them off before they reached their car.

"Good Morning, Keisha. I'm so glad I caught you before you got away for the day."

Keisha didn't know this man, but she smiled and stopped since he called her name. "Good Morning."

"We've never met, but I'm Jackson Gooding. I was Laura's friend. I met Carlton, but I never met you. I would like to talk to Carlton, if you don't mind. Is he in?"

"He goes to work around ten, so he's not up yet. Why don't you call him later?"

"I don't have his number. Can you give it to me?" Jackson knew how to turn on the charm. He hoped Keisha would trust him enough to give him the number. She did. She gave him Carlton's mobile number and work number.

"Thanks, Keisha. I know you working moms have to get going in the morning. I don't want to make you late." He helped her with getting the baby into his car seat, and held her car door while they said goodbye. He didn't want her to know he wouldn't leave until he saw Carlton.

Jackson settled into his car again. This time he allowed himself to nap until about nine. He thought by then Carlton would be up and getting dressed. When he rang the doorbell, he listened for movement inside the bungalow. He could hear a television and someone approaching the door. Jackson stepped back, expecting the door to open. He knew Carlton had to be on the other side of the door watching him through the peephole. When the door didn't open, Jackson knocked, and said, "Carlton, it's me. I know you're in there."

Carlton opened the door, looking down at his feet.

Jackson extended his hand to shake it. "Hey, man. I'm so sorry about your mom. When Angela told me, I took the first flight I could get."

Carlton still stood in the doorway, not motioning for Jackson to come in.

"Can I come in? I know you have to go to work, so I won't take too much of your time." Carlton let him in, and led him into the kitchen, where Carlton had been eating a bowl of cereal.

"Tell me what happened. How did she die?" Jackson asked.

Carlton held his forehead, and shook his head. "Man, I didn't want to have to tell you. I don't know where Mom is."

He dug into a kitchen drawer and pulled out a piece of paper. "I came home and found this note in her handwriting." He showed it to Jackson.

"That's her writing all right."

Carlton, I need to get away. You can let the site die when the hosting bill comes due. Tell them I died, I don't care.

"I haven't heard from her," Carlton began. "She left her cell phone, her Corvette is parked in her space at the condo, but she took clothes. I don't know what to do. When I called Ms. Angela, I wanted to tell her, ask her to help find Mom, but I didn't know what to do. It just came out all wrong and I sounded stupid."

Now Jackson had to regroup. Laura's not dead, but she's missing.

"Ok Carlton, when did this happen? When did she leave?"

"It's been two weeks." Carlton said.

"Did you go to the police?"

"What would I tell the police? 'My mom ran away from home?' She's done 'get-aways' before. They wouldn't think it was anything to be concerned about, but I know this time is different." Carlton said, "This time she hasn't called. This time she didn't leave me any money."

"Do you think we should call it a 'Silver Alert?'" Jackson asked.

"Mom would hate being called a senior."

"She's over fifty, she has a heart condition, and you don't know where she is. Look, I'll go with you to the police. You need to get a recent photo."

"I need to go to work. Can we do this later?" Jackson could hear the little boy in him trying to dodge.

"Carlton, we have taken too long with this. Call in sick, or whatever. We need to do this."

* * * *

It was Tuesday night before Jackson called Angela with the news.

"Angela, girl, I hope you're sitting down."

"Oh, no, it can't be more bad news."

"It's good news and bad news. Which one do you want first?"

"Don't play with me, Jackson, just tell me."

Jackson relented. "The good news is Laura didn't die like Carlton told you. The bad news is we don't know where she is."

He told her all the details, and how long it took to convince the police to file a missing persons report. They were able to get it filed as a Silver Alert. The local news stations were already showing Laura's photo.

"My goodness, Jackson, it makes more sense now, but how will we ever find her?"

"That's the thing," Jackson said. "She's a grown woman. She can disappear if she wants to. Carlton and I had to tell the police she was suffering from depression and we were concerned about her safety. With her heart condition, she needs to be with someone who can help her in the case of an emergency. But if we want to find her, it's back on you now, Angela. You need to get the Silver Alert broadcast all over the country, all over the world."

Angela thought for a minute and said, "We do have a network of friends. The Meet & Greet group on Facebook has over a thousand members, a good number of them outside the United States. But do you or Carlton have any idea where she might have gone? We can post the Silver Alert on all the websites we go to, but it needs to be broadcast on TV to get the proper attention. How do you propose we get that kind of coverage?"

Jackson was stoked, "Can't you get that Meet & Greet group to do the foot work...get that thing to their local police and TV stations?"

Angela was up to the challenge. "Get Carlton to email me Laura's photo and the alert. How is he taking all this attention? He was afraid to go public, wasn't he?"

"I don't know if he was so much afraid, as he was slow to get moving," Jackson said. "When I left him tonight, he thanked me for coming and getting involved."

"When are you going back home? I hope you get some sleep before you make that trip."

"I'll call tonight to see when I can go. I might have to go check on Bonita before I go."

"I thought you said she was a freak," Angela said.

"Well, she's a good cook, and if that Stacey isn't around, I can control the situation."

"Sure you can. Be safe, Jackson."

Angela got busy online, posting an update on Laura. She knew TheGuy would be the first to say, "Didn't I tell you." But she hoped she could make people understand the situation was still serious. Certainly Laura had a right to go away if she wanted, but Angela questioned her state of mind. Whatever Jackson and Carlton told the police was not stretching the truth.

This was one of those times when Angela sat back and let the discussion go on without jumping in. She needed the help of the friends who wanted to find Laura. The private messages started to come in. Angela started a list of people who wanted to help in the Washington, DC area, New York City, Miami, Chicago, and Los Angeles. The only person to volunteer from abroad was in Sydney. Angela thanked Camellia for volunteering, but she thought it was a stretch for Laura to make it to Australia. Camellia insisted she could reach thousands of people with her travels and her own radio broadcast. One of the members who had a page on Facebook said he would create a "Find Laura" page.

When Bodine came in from his garden with a load of green beans, she bubbled over with the news.

"I get it, Angela. You have to do this. But don't stretch yourself too much. You talk about Laura's health. You're older than she is."

"But I take care of myself. Laura smokes. I work out." Angela flexed her biceps for him.

"Okay Mrs. Obama. You know I'm going to step in if I see you dragging yourself around."

"I love you, Sweetie. The sight of all those green beans is making me tired already." Angela knew how to get out of doing too much work in the kitchen. Standing in the kitchen made her side ache, but she sat down and watched while Bodine snapped the green beans. She thought about those measurements she had to learn in elementary school. "Exactly how big would a bushel of green beans be? Or is it a peck." Whatever it was, they both knew when those beans cooked in their biggest pot, Bodine would fill up a few quart containers for the freezer.

They weren't thinking much about Laura when the phone rang. The annoying voice announced a New York City number that Angela didn't recognize.

"Angelplaits. It's Harman...you know, Kareem's brother. I don't spend a lot of time on Blaq-Kawfee, but people have been calling me all afternoon about Laura. I don't know if she told you, but we had a thing going when she wasn't talking to Jackson."

"No, I didn't know," Angela said. "But you know how QTEE was, always talking about some man. I never knew what was real with her. But have you heard she is missing?"

"Girl, I heard she was dead. And then I got a message from her on my voicemail. I was so spooked, I near 'bout dropped the phone. My phone was off when she called, so I didn't see the Caller ID, and she didn't leave a number. So you're telling me she's missing. After I got all those phone calls, I knew if anybody knew anything, you would."

"What did she say in her message?" Angela asked.

"She said she needed to see me and she was tired of this mess. Then she said she'd call me when she got there. I tried calling the number I had for her, but it went straight to voicemail."

"You know you can get the calling number from your voicemail. There should be an option for 'get envelope information.' I have to get my phone and walk you through what it says on my phone."

After several minutes of going through voicemail menu choices, Harman had the phone number Laura had used. He lost the connection with Angela in the process, but he called back.

"I tried that number, and it went straight to voicemail," Harman said.

"What time did you get the call?"

"It was on my phone when I turned it on this morning."

"Do you think she might be in New York?" Angela asked.

"I wondered that myself. I'll call her number again and leave a message. I'm worried about her. Her voice didn't sound right. She was out of breath, like she had been running or something. I don't know where she might be if she is in New York. She had some bad blood with family members. The family of her ex lives here, and they were nothing but trouble."

Harman continued, "But, you know it's like Laura to run away, and not know where she was going."

"I'm afraid for her. I'm worried she might do something dangerous. Do you know any of her family you could call?"

"I have a couple of names. I'll make some calls and see what I come up with. But she said she would call back. I'll have to leave my phone on."

When Angela finally hung up, Bodine gave her a worried look. He had heard enough from Angela's side of the conversation to know what it was about. "Still playing sleuth, aren't you?"

"What do you think I should do, let it be?"

"Angela, she's a grown woman. She can travel where she wants to."

"But she sounds desperate. She left the message for her son to tell them she's dead, and she didn't tell him where she was going."

"What are you going to do while we're on our South American cruise next week?" Bodine asked. "I'm glad all these people don't have your cell phone number. You would be racking up international roaming minutes. Promise me you will let it go long enough to enjoy the trip."

"You're right. I promise. I need to get my clothes out to pack."

Angela wondered how she could organize her one bag while she was still preoccupied with finding Laura. Bodine would never understand why she worried so much. She knew it would be difficult to put Laura's issues on the backburner, and make her husband her priority. But she did promise.

CHAPTER FOUR

Wednesday

Angela received an email from Carlton with the Silver Alert and photo attached. Angela hardly recognized the Laura she saw in the photo. On the two times they had met, Laura was petite and thin. She used to complain about not having any *"tatas."* Every photo she posted on the website was of the same petite woman. This photo showed someone who was thirty pounds heavier, plump and smiling.

It was still early, but she had to call Jackson on his cell phone.

"Woman, do you know what time it is?"

"Uh, it depends on where you are." Angela said. "I guess I called too early. Where are you?"

"It's five a.m. in Las Vegas. Since I'm wide awake now, what's up?"

"I got this photo from Carlton. You saw it, didn't you? How long has Laura been fat?"

Jackson chuckled, "Oh she was proud of that photo. When she

sent it to me, she said, 'Now I have some boobs.'"

"But she must have gained thirty pounds in the last year. It can't be healthy to gain so much in a year."

"It was probably the medications she took, or so she said."

"I guess I'm getting too involved in this," Angela said, "but I wonder if she took her meds with her."

"Carlton said she didn't."

"You didn't put it in this Silver Alert message. Do you think I should get a list of her meds from Carlton? I could ask my doctor what the consequences would be if she missed her meds for a few weeks."

"I'm sure he would give it to you," Jackson said, "but don't call him for another three hours. He doesn't have to be at work until ten."

Angela busied herself with getting her suitcases out of the attic and printing out her packing list for the trip. She and Bodine cruised so often she had it down to a routine. This trip would require two seasons of clothes, cold in Chile and warm in Brazil. Bodine had managed to get all of his clothes in one bag under fifty pounds. Angela thought she would be able to do the same if she packed only two pairs of shoes, one for evening and a pair of sandals. She would travel in her sneakers and wear them for the walking tours. Otherwise she would pack lightweight shirts for layers instead of taking heavy sweaters; she might have to purchase a second bag to return home. They couldn't go all the way around Cape Horn and not bring home some Chilean sweaters and wine.

She managed to stay off the website until afternoon. There were over twenty people online at once, unusually high for a weekday. The forums were buzzing with the news that Laura had gone missing. Most people weren't taking it seriously. Some were calling her the "Runaway Bride."

When Harman showed up on BK, he spent some time greeting people he had not chatted with in weeks. He joined in the discussions about Laura. Before Angela knew it, there were twenty people in the chat room. Angela could never focus when there were too many people typing at once, and she gave up trying to see if Harman said he had heard from Laura. It was clear the other women were enjoying the drama, goaded on by "TheGuy."

When Angela received the email from Carlton with the list of Laura's meds, she decided to Google the names rather than ask her doctor what they were. Three of them were heart medicines. No surprise there. And there was one for diabetes. Angela had never known Laura was diabetic, but she knew if Laura went without her meds, she could be in serious trouble. There was one for depression and another for mood swings.

She called Jackson on his mobile number.

"Whatchu got this time?" Jackson asked.

"Did you know Laura was diabetic?"

"Hmmm. She never told me what meds she was taking. She told me about the heart issues. She had a couple of heart surgeries I knew about. In the times we were together, I never saw her checking her blood sugar. You would think after five years, I would know this. But I guess it was easy to stay in a fantasy when we didn't see each other in person enough."

Angela wondered if she should mention the call from Harman, or let Jackson read it on Blaq-Kawfee. Jackson didn't get online often, so she decided to let it slide.

"I think I'll update the Alert on Blaq-Kawfee to say she left without her medication. I've already told more of her business than she might want. Look, we're going out of town for a couple of weeks. Leaving on Friday morning."

"Are you cruising again?" Jackson asked.

"Yes, two weeks in South America."

"Y'all sure know how to live."

"You have my email address, don't you?" Angela said. She made sure she had Jackson's current email. "Email me if you get any new information. I don't expect I'll hear anything while I'm gone. Are you still in Vegas?"

"I may stay another day or so, checking out the casinos."

"You and Bonita?"

"Listen, Angela. Life is short, and Laura dumped me. I still love her, and I want her to be safe. Besides, Bonita is a good cook."

"I hear you. Be careful out there, and let me know if you hear anything. You don't get online much do you, anymore?"

"No," Jackson said. "Besides, Blaq-Kawfee will be history by the time you get back. Where will I find you online now?"

"Stay in touch with me by email until we know more," Angela

said.

When Angela signed back online, she saw the discussion about Laura had settled down, but there was a new thread entitled, "Time for Facebook." TheGuy had started the thread. He knew how Laura financed the site and suspected Blaq-Kawfee would be gone by the end of the month.

"Post your Facebook names here, so we can keep up after Blaq-Kawfee dies."

Forty-five members had posted the "government names" they used on Facebook. Most people were known everywhere by a single screen name, but Facebook wanted a real name when you signed up. Some people used Facebook with a variation of their screen name. To show solidarity, Angela posted her name, Angela Platte Beaudoin. Bodine had already set up his Facebook as Bodine Fuerst. *Where did he get such a name?*

The next time the phone rang it was Shannon from Los Angeles. Angela talked to her on the phone from time to time, and Bodine had already planned to meet Shannon and her husband when they stopped over on the way to South America.

"Hi Angela. I know you're following all the drama on the site about QTEE."

"Girl, you don't know the half. But I'm trying to step back for a bit since we have this trip coming up."

"Harman called us after he talked to you," Shannon said. "He's concerned about Laura. He's been calling people all over New York asking if they have heard anything. None of her relatives were the least bit concerned. I think they all wrote her off after she moved to Las Vegas. Harman knows I couldn't care less. QTEE never liked me anyway. She liked to warn Harman about 'that white girl.' She thought I stole Kareem from her."

"But I thought she and Harman were a thing when it wasn't Jackson. You're losing me here."

"Too much drama, I know. I know you and Bodine try to stay out of it."

"Anyway, we'll be flying into LA on Saturday. Are you going to be able to meet us at our hotel?" Angela asked. "It will be good to see you"

"Yes we're looking forward to it."

OK Shannon, I'll see you online, and on Saturday. You have my cell number."

Angela went back to packing. The phone announced a call from Harman.

"I heard from Laura," Harman said. "She called me from JFK airport."

"So she's in New York. What is she going to do? Where is she staying?"

"She's not staying. She was about to board a flight to Rio."

"Rio? Who does she know in Rio?" Angela asked.

"Now I didn't ask her. The only way I ever managed to get along with QTEE was to ask no questions, just let her talk."

"So did she tell you anything?"

"She went on and on about Jackson and how they broke up.

How he was so insecure, controlling….yada yada. She said she needed to clear her head, and Rio was one of the places on her bucket list."

"Any idea why she was in New York?" Angela asked.

"She said something about going to her old doctor. Some quack who would give her any meds she wanted."

"Oh no, do you think she's taking something dangerous?"

"I asked her how she felt." Harman said avoiding Angela's question.

"And…"

"She said she hadn't been checking her blood sugar, and the doctor wanted to put her in the hospital to get her stabilized. She spent one night in a hospital here. Said it was the best rest she'd had in months. She got all her prescriptions and she was all set for Rio."

"Any idea where she might be staying in Rio? We'll be cruising South America out of Chile. We don't get to Rio until the second week," Angela said.

"She said she would figure it all out after she gets there. You know she claimed to be fluent in five languages. Says she speaks Portuguese. Look, what is the best way to get in touch with you while you're away?"

"The best way is my email. We use the internet cafe onboard the ship and get to an internet café in the ports if we have time. Let me know anything you hear from QTEE. Give me her phone number. She might answer a call from me. She has so many email addresses I never knew how to contact her except by phone. And look...are you on Facebook? The gang from Blaq-Kawfee is set to keep the discussion going on Facebook. We expect the site to fold at the end of the month."

"OK, I'll get on Facebook...something else I have to figure out. But I will email you with anything I hear." Harman said before he gave Angela the phone number.

Angela planned what she would say when she called Laura, and wondered if Laura would answer her call.

CHAPTER FIVE

Thursday Morning

Angela got up early to get to her last spinning class before the cruise. The 7:30 class was generally brutal.

"Why do you put yourself through a spinning class?" Bodine asked. "You always come home limping."

"I feel like I really had a workout after Alison's class. I like to get a cycle in the middle where she can't see me." She snickered. "Alison likes to try to intimidate people into pumping harder than they want to. I don't hurt myself, but my legs feel like they're going to give out after the class...gotta get going."

Angela worked up a good sweat in her cycling class. She never thought about anything when she was cycling, other than trying to keep pace with the class of younger women. Most classes could be divided into two groups, the jocks and the senior citizens. Alison liked to call people out if they weren't keeping up. "Why do you bother coming to this class if you're not going to push yourself?"

Alison would say. Angela knew her own limits. Some days her knees started screaming when she walked up the steps to spinning class. She wasn't going to risk injuring herself.

She went home to shower and change, and to check her email. Angela found it difficult to do only one task on the computer without going to the Blaq-Kawfee site.

"I'll take one peek to see what the top discussion topics are today," she said to herself. There were eight people on the site. She hadn't told anyone QTEE had made contact, but she didn't want to get sucked into a discussion. She didn't see anything posted by Harman.

Angela didn't usually wait until the last minute to pack although she was never as early as Bodine. They would be leaving early on Saturday, and Angela had only laid out a few dresses for eveningwear. She needed to launder some jeans and shirts for daytime wear.

"Now I need to get my packing organized. Charge the MP3 player, Camera, Mini. Line up meds for eighteen days. One pair of dress shoes, sandals, rubber shoes, and I'll travel in the sneakers," she said to herself.

QTEE may have landed in Rio by now. Let me try once to call. QTEE's phone rang five times and went to voicemail. *She must be there with the phone on.*

"Laura, it's me Angela. Harman gave me this number and said you were going to Rio. We'll be in Rio in a couple of weeks. We're sailing from Chile around Cape Horn. Call me please. I'm worried about you." Angela tried not to sound panicky. She wanted to keep it low-key so QTEE might call her back.

By the time Bodine was back from his errands, Angela had laid out all her clothes and was checking off her list. She often thought about taking the same outfits from one cruise to the next, but this time they would have a couple of climate changes. Besides, although the others on the cruise wouldn't care what they wore, Angela liked their trip photos to show different clothes.

She sent out her usual email to family, making sure they knew how to reach them in case of emergency. Angela planned to take her cell phone, and arranged for international roaming at the port stops. She reminded the family that they could reach her and Bodine by email when phoning wasn't possible. She made her round of phone calls to make sure her older siblings had what they needed while she was gone.

She still had to pick up a few things from the grocery store for her oldest sister Maxine and her husband Leo at their apartment in the retirement community. There was usually something she needed to adjust for them in their apartment when she went to check on them. When Leo told her the apartment was always too hot, Angela reminded him to keep Maxine away from the thermostat. And she showed them again how to make phone calls using the address book she had set up on their cordless phone, reminding them still again to press OFF when they finished the call. They were still leaving the phone on at least once a week. Those times, someone from the front desk would have to go upstairs to their apartment to turn the phone off.

By late afternoon, Angela had finished her rounds, and was pleased Bodine had pulled out all the leftovers to put together dinner for the two of them.

"Thank you, Sweetie. What would I do without you?"

"You sure wouldn't starve, with all we have in the freezer," Bodine said. Angela chuckled at his sarcasm.

Angela had all her clothes packed before she turned in Thursday night. She had a few spare minutes to check in online to see if there was any news on Laura. TheGuy had started a discussion thread titled "QTEE's Men - Speak up." Angela was afraid to see who responded. There were a dozen responses from women on the site, who took it to be another one of TheGuy's jokes, and kidded him for trying to start something. All the men on the site little by little responded with kind comments about what Laura meant to them. Paulo from Brazil was online. There were people from all over the country who said how QTEE had touched their lives. There were musicians and rappers from California, Delaware, and New York who said how QTEE had encouraged them in their music, and bought their CDs. Soleman and Winmyheart couldn't imagine what their days would be like without BK. And there was Camellia from Australia, her aborigine friend who had once come all the way to the States and attended a Meet & Greet in DC. When she posted a topic about what to do with skin tags, it was an epiphany for a lot of people including Angela, when she learned indigenous people all over the world often have the same health issues. Acousticsoul brought her quiet spirit to the forums. She didn't have a photograph on her page, and Angela never knew her real name. Discussions with her were thought provoking and none of the usual relationship questions Angela stayed away from. Acousticsoul wrote a poem for QTEE and her memories of her.

Angela started tearing up from reading it. She hated to think it would all be gone, and never seen by QTEE before the site shut down, so she copied the whole thread and saved it to her PC. The end of the month would pass while they were gone on the cruise, and tonight might be her last chance to save some of the memories of Blaq-Kawfee.

Friday

Angela and Bodine arrived in LA around noon Pacific Time. When they reached their hotel, Angela called Shannon on her cell phone.

"I can hardly wait to see you," Shannon said. "Kareem is helping me get Anika ready so she can ride with us. We'll get there around five, and take you out to dinner."

Shannon's daughter had a spinal cord injury from an automobile accident five years ago. She and Kareem were married soon after the accident. Kareem loved her so much he wanted to help her through those long months when Anika was hospitalized for multiple surgeries, and finally had rehab so she could come home. Theirs was one of those internet relationships that worked.

"We're excited about seeing you this time, too." The last time Angela and Bodine came through LA, Kareem met them and had lunch before they continued on a train trip across country. Shannon wasn't able to come that time due to a family emergency. "We're going to bump around here near the park until we can get into our hotel room. We'll have time for a nap before you pick us up."

"See you later, Angelplaits," Shannon said.

When Shannon and Kareem arrived in Los Angeles, Angela was refreshed from a nap, and raced downstairs to meet them when she received their call. She and Bodine saw the van coming up to the front of the hotel, but Shannon was nowhere in sight.

Kareem laughed. "She thought she could go inside and find you. She couldn't sit still."

When Shannon appeared from the other side of the building, she and Angela ran to meet each other and hugged and danced like old friends. Anybody watching would never guess they were seeing each other in the flesh for the first time.

Angela had an ongoing joke about who had the biggest butt, and laughed that Shannon had her beat. "Of course, you are taller than I imagined." Shannon was close to six feet, which didn't seem so tall when she stood next to her husband who was six-five. This was a rare time for Angela to feel petite.

Shannon had it all planned to take them out to dinner at a steak and seafood restaurant. Anika could access the whole outdoor mall in her wheelchair. She smiled and shook hands when they met her, but she didn't have much to say afterwards. Angela watched how Shannon babied her daughter, adjusting her in her chair, feeding her, and holding her cup to drink. Angela thought how well her son Stephen managed on his own although she knew Anika's injury made her quadriplegic. Only a matter of inches on the spinal cord made the difference between Stephen being paraplegic and Anika being a quadriplegic. She and Bodine had talked often about how parents of disabled children needed to prepare for the time when the parent would no longer be able to take care of the child. Angela wished Shannon could help her daughter become independent or at least live in a setting where Shannon would not feel required to be with her every day. Bodine had a way of reading Angela's expression, knowing what she was thinking. As Angela was about to say to Shannon, "What would Anika..." Bodine kicked her under the table. She knew he thought she was getting into other people's business again, so Angela shut up.

It was easier to dive into the questions about QTEE. Kareem had not talked to his brother in New York, so Angela had to get him caught up. Kareem gave Shannon an endearing look and changed the subject. QTEE was not a subject Shannon cared to talk about.

CHAPTER SIX

Saturday, March 22

Saturday morning, Angela and Bodine took the hotel shuttle to the airport for their flight to Valparaiso, Chile. Angela was still jet-lagged from the flight to LA, and slept through the flight to Chile. Bodine was prepared to purchase their visas when they went through customs in Chile. It wasn't fair how the Brazilian consulate required them to jump through hoops to get visas weeks in advance for the mere two port stops they would have in Brazil.

Angela and Bodine liked to have a boarding photo from all their cruises and would often dress alike for the photo. This time they both wore their Royal Caribbean t-shirts with the word "Crew" across the front. After they left their luggage with the attendants and started to enter the check-in area, one of the crew members tried to direct them to the crew entrance. Angela thought it was hysterical at the idea of two gray-haired sexagenarians mistaken for crew. They ignored the crew member who didn't understand

English, and proceeded to the door for passengers. Otherwise, the check in for the cruise was smooth as usual with the express line for Gold level Crown and Anchor members. Angela snickered when they called them Mr. & Mrs. Beaudoin, pronounced the French way. Bodine's family came from the Gulf Coast of Mississippi, and none of them spoke French.

The first day of the cruise, the Beaudoin's routine was the same as with every one of their twenty-some cruises. They had lunch in the Windjammer, the name Royal Caribbean gives its buffet restaurant. They dropped their carry-on luggage in the cabin after the cabin stewards opened the door to their hallway signaling the cabins were cleared. Bodine had ordered flowers in advance for Angela to have in the cabin. In addition, this time he had stashed Easter candy in his carry-on for Angela to have a supply of Peeps and jelly beans. They continued with an exploration of the ship, taking pictures of all the public areas, so they would have a complete set to share with their family and friends. Bodine had to check with the main dining room to locate their assigned table. He had requested a table for two, and got his wish most of the time. This time they discovered theirs was a table for six, and they waited in the line to have it changed, but there were no remaining tables for two.

They spent the few hours before dinner, relaxing in the cabin until the crew delivered their luggage and they could unpack. At dinner they met their assigned tablemates, two couples from Quebec. One of the women, Susanne, was fluent in French and

English, both of the men spoke some English, and the other woman spoke little English. They were pleasant enough. Susanne did a lot of translating back and forth to get through the introductions, but then they settled into talking amongst themselves in French.

By the end of dinner, Bodine whispered to Angela, "I wonder if my French name put us at this table." Angela had to snicker. Bodine had a talk with the maître d' after the meal and had their table changed. The next day they had three nice ladies from Maryland as their tablemates. The sixth seat at the table was assigned to a friend of the three ladies who preferred to eat in the Windjammer buffet because she thought the main dining room was too fancy.

Bodine, who had lived most of his life in the DC / Maryland area, was especially happy to have tablemates who knew the same parks, restaurants, shopping malls, and entertainment venues he grew up with. The ladies were also Federal government retirees, just as Bodine was. He talked so much that night at dinner he remembered why he preferred a table for two, where he and Angela could finish dinner more quickly.

* * * *

Angela had not realized they would be cruising on Easter until she looked at the calendar for March. It was an early Easter Sunday, March 23. Bodine booked their trips months, often a year in advance. While Angela spent her time on Blaq-Kawfee, Bodine would troll cruise line websites looking for a good deal on a cruise.

This cruise was $400 cheaper per person than the ones before or after, because of Easter. Angela couldn't remember an Easter when she wasn't in church for either the sunrise service or the regular morning service. This Easter she stood on the pool deck of the Splendour of the Seas, off the coast of Chile. The sea was so rough the pool had waves sloshing back and forth, wetting the deck. Their itinerary included stops in Chile, cruising through the Chilean Fjords, and around Cape Horn. All those days at sea would be restful. There was no better sleeping than on a rocking ship. Angela had brought a few books along, and those afternoons at sea, she could be found on a deck somewhere, wrapped in a blanket, with her nodding head on her chest. Angela almost put QTEE out of her mind.

Sunday Morning in Las Vegas

A tall male nurse entered Jackson's hospital room as the sunlight was coming through the window.

"Good morning, Mr. Gooding, are you awake from the dead? It's a beautiful Easter Sunday morning."

Jackson barely peeped through his eyelids when he tried to respond, "Mmmp nnn."

Oh no, my tongue is so swollen I can't talk.

He looked around the room and then to his body, taking in the IV dripping into his right arm, the blood pressure cuff on his left, wires stuck to his chest and legs for an EKG, and a damn catheter.

How did I get here?

He tried talking again, sounding like a cartoon dog. "Rmph rrlll."

"Don't try to talk Mr. Gooding. You had an allergic reaction.

"I asked that woman if the gumbo had shellfish in it. She lied! I never had a reaction this bad before."

"It's a good thing your lady took good care of you. When you collapsed, she took you to the ER right away. She thought you had stopped breathing. And the medics had difficulty giving you CPR. A gentleman your age, you have to be cautious. We had to put your medication in the IV. After the doctor sees you, he may remove the IV."

My lady, my ass. That Bonita.

Jackson pretended to write on his hand, and let out a loud doggy sound.

"Oh sure, you can write." Then the nurse gave him a pad and pen.

Jackson wrote, "I have to get out of here. I live in Memphis."

"Sir, you have been sleeping since Friday night, and the doctor will have to see you on his rounds."

And it's Sunday morning? I missed a whole day. Where is Bonita?

He wrote, "I just met the lady a few days ago. She has to get me out of here. Where are my things?"

"Don't you worry. She said she would hold your wallet and keys."

"What about my phone? I need to find someone." Jackson wrote.

"Sir, lie back and let me get your vital signs. You can't go anywhere without someone to help you."

Jackson relented, letting the nurse take his temperature, check his blood pressure, prick his finger. When the nurse had finished, an orderly arrived with a tray. Jackson realized he was hungry, but didn't know how he could manage eating. The tray contained breakfast, a soft diet. Jackson sipped his juice through a straw and nibbled at the scrambled eggs. His tongue would not cooperate, but he managed to get all of the egg and gelatin down. The nurse had left by then.

Jackson decided he would get out of bed. Once he pulled off the blood pressure cuff, the monitor started beeping and the nurse came back.

"Mr. Gooding, you have to rest until the doctor sees you."

Jackson grabbed his notepad again. "I need to see if I can stand."

The nurse decided to help him by removing the other monitors and the catheter. Jackson felt tired again after so much activity. This time he wrote, "Let me lie back for a minute. Can you get me my phone?"

Once he had the phone, Jackson realized he wouldn't be able to talk into it anyway. In addition, he had never sent a text message in his life. The nurse was gone again. Jackson would have to get someone to make the call for him. Damn. He hated feeling so helpless. But he tried again to stand up, holding onto the rolling stand for the IV. He swayed and rocked, but he was able to walk to the chair and sit.

A woman came into the room and introduced herself as the hospital social worker, Karen Stewart. She gave her prepared speech about being an advocate for all their Medicare patients. Jackson's mind started to wander as he wondered how the hospital had gotten his Medicare information.

"Mr. Gooding, we want to make sure you are satisfied with your treatment and you aren't sent home before you can take care of yourself."

Jackson had his note pad with him and wrote, "I live in Memphis and I need help to get home."

Ms. Stewart didn't have a script prepared for Jackson's circumstance, and while she stumbled with an answer, Jackson shoved another note at her. "I have to check out of a hotel and return a rental car. I don't know where my wallet is."

"Mr. Gooding, if you can't talk, you need someone to help you with those things."

Jackson wanted to write, "DUH." But he wrote, "That's what I'm trying to tell you."

"Don't you have some family here in Las Vegas?"

Jackson started fumbling with his cell phone, and found Bonita's phone number. He motioned to Ms. Stewart to call the number.

"Is this Bonita? I'm the hospital social worker at University Medical Center. I have Jackson Gooding here who asked me to call you to help him...No he still can't talk...Yes, the hotel. You have his suitcase? Returned the car? I'll tell him."

"Did you hear that, Mr. Gooding?" Ms. Stewart asked as she gave Jackson his phone back. "Your friend has taken care of all the details, and she's coming to the hospital this afternoon. She said she had to go to church. It's Easter, you know. Now you should get back in the bed and rest."

Jackson was relieved. He was so sure Bonita had gone off with his wallet and left him with no way to get home. He allowed Ms. Stewart to help him back to the bed. He was exhausted and fell back into a deep sleep.

CHAPTER SEVEN

Touring South America

The first port stop in Chile was Puerto Montt where they had a tour and a history lesson of Chile. Angela and Bodine never realized Germans had been invited to settle in the southern region of Chile in the nineteenth century, and there was significant evidence of German culture. Angela studied German years ago in college, and was puzzled when they saw a sign hanging in a house they toured from the colonial period reading, "*Der Herr lasse sein Angesicht leuchten uber dir.*" She took a photograph of the sign and decided she would figure it out later. She knew Herr meant *man*, mister, or *sir*. Then it came to her later this was Biblical language, from the Book of Numbers. "The Lord let his face to shine upon you." All the frenzy she had felt about QTEE went away and she felt peace wash over her.

When they returned from the tour and changed clothes, Angela and Bodine had a pleasant dinner in the main dining room. They had chosen the early seating, which on other cruises would be at 6:00, but for this itinerary ending in Brazil, the early seating was 7:30 to conform to the late dinner preferences of most Brazilians. Angela groaned the first night. She wanted to prevent any chance of reflux from eating too close to bedtime. She and Bodine saw some advantage of the later hour as they strolled around the ship after dinner. They stopped to listen to the Splendour of the Seas Dance Band in the Centrum, and found a comfortable seat to people-watch and have a glass of wine. When the band started playing Fleetwood Mac's "Don't Stop...thinking about tomorrow," Angela felt a little bit of a buzz, and although she wasn't a particular fan of Fleetwood Mac, the beat sounded good, so she grabbed Bodine's hand.

"Let's dance."

Most nights on past cruises the action didn't get started until after ten and Bodine complained they missed the dance party because they were too sleepy to stay up with nothing to do between dinner and the ten o'clock disc jockey. Nobody else was dancing in the Centrum, but once Angela and Bodine were out there doing what Bodine called "hand dancing," other couples joined in. When the band finished their set, they thanked the audience in the Centrum for dancing to their music.

The next day they cruised through the Chilean Fjords. It reminded Angela of the glaciers they had seen in Alaska on their honeymoon cruise. Two days of cruising gave them plenty of napping time. Some folks were on deck trying to get a suntan, but it was too chilly in Chile for Angela and Bodine. They were happy to dock in Punta Arenas where they bought sweaters hand-knitted from alpaca. Bodine added his sweater as another layer under his super warm hoodie from Jasper Canada.

Angela checked her email while on the ship. One of the perks of being in the Crown & Anchor Society was ten dollars worth of free internet. At fifty cents a minute, ten dollars would buy twenty minutes. Twenty minutes by satellite on a moving ship allowed her to check her email and not read anything unless it was an emergency. She saw nothing from Jackson and nothing from Harman.

The exciting part of the trip started in Argentina, Puerto Madryn and Buenos Aires with their neighborhoods of corrugated metal houses painted in all the colors of the rainbow. And tango dancers. It didn't take much for street entrepreneurs to break into dance and look for a tip from tourists. On a stop from a tour in Buenos Aires, one dancer grabbed Bodine, wrapped one leg around him and placed a hat on his head in a pose for a photo. After Angela snapped the photo, the dancer retrieved her hat and looked for Bodine to thank her with a tip. He was grinning too much about the pose he couldn't refuse a tip. It used to bother Angela when she saw graffiti all over cities, on historic buildings, churches, museums, but she had come to accept it as a sign of the times, and not solely a phenomenon of ghettos in the USA. They visited the cemetery and saw the crypt of Eva Peron.

Angela turned her cell phone on in the ports long enough to

receive any messages. There were a few text messages from family members, but nothing about Laura. She thought Jackson would have checked in with her by now. He knew she was on a cruise, but Angela had not told him about Laura's going to Rio. Angela wanted to hear from Laura first.

Evenings aboard ship reflected the fun people were having on shore. One night another band was playing music from Argentina, a song it seemed everyone knew. They were in the Centrum again looking down from the third level, and people were singing along in Spanish from three levels of the Centrum. Angela recorded a video on her digital camera, and promised herself she would learn enough Spanish to understand the song.

Another week goes by

They arrived in Rio on Saturday the fourteenth day of the cruise. Bodine had picked a city tour including Sugar Loaf, Christ the Redeemer, and ending with a meal at a steak house. When they arrived in port, Angela turned on her phone, hoping for a message from QTEE. Since there wasn't she took a chance on calling.

Angela was shocked when QTEE answered, "Hello Beautiful."

"Girl, you don't know how worried I have been about you."

"What's up?" Laura asked.

"You go off and tell Carlton to say you're dead."

"He didn't really do that, did he?"

"YAH. You need to call your son and let him know you're all right."

"OK, Momma. I'll do that. Are you happy now?" Laura asked.

Angela said, "We're here in Rio. Is there any chance we could see you?"

"Where are you?" Laura asked.

Angela heard the impatience in her voice, but she told Laura about the tour from the cruise ship.

"What time do you think you'll be at the statue...you know, Christ the Redeemer?" Laura was still being abrupt.

"I don't know, and I don't think the guide can tell us. There are twenty-some buses leaving the port in a minute...I need to get on bus number eight. They're doing variations of the same tour, and the guides change the order of their stops to avoid having traffic jams with too many buses arriving at the same place at the same time."

Then Laura said, "I tell you what. Look for me near the statue. You'll see me."

"It's a good thing I got a recent picture of you, or I would never be able to recognize you. I'm wearing a red baseball cap from Finland. How will I find you?"

"Cap from Finland?"

"Don't ask...but how...?"

"Don't worry...you'll see me," Laura insisted.

Bodine was getting antsy. He liked to be one of the first ones on the bus so they could get a seat near the back door. Angela had to run to catch up.

"I talked to QTEE. She's going to meet us at the Christ the

Redeemer statue."

Bodine sighed. "Is she OK?"

"She sounds like she always does...kind of flaky. You know how she can say one thing but it sounds like she means something else."

"Whatever." Bodine said. "Let's get on the bus."

The tour showed them the best and worst of Rio, including the colorful hillside slums like boxcars piled on top of each other on the hillsides. Their guide commented how the government had a plan to move the poorest people from the slums to housing projects further away from the city. The intent was to improve the slums, but it meant that those in the housing projects would not have access to public transportation to jobs in the city. When they reached the tram to take them to the top of Sugarloaf Mountain, the weather was still cloudy and damp. On reaching the top, they were above the clouds as the sky started to clear for a breathtaking view. Their guide had given them one hour to get back to the bus. They had time to stand in line for a potty break, take photos of the view from Christ the Redeemer, and shop for souvenirs.

Angela decided not to say anything about looking for QTEE, and stay with Bodine taking pictures. He had taken photos of the statue from a distance, and now they were at the summit where all the tourists gathered at the feet of Cristo Redentor, like bees on a honey bun. It was impossible to get a photo without thirty of your closest bus-mates. Bodine hated it, but he took what photos he could.

Bodine brought it up first. "Do you see her? Where did she say she would be? What time?"

"She didn't give a time, and I couldn't tell her what time we might get here. She just said, 'You'll see me'."

They continued taking pictures of the statue and of the view and went into the gift shop. Bodine looked for refrigerator magnets to take home, something he did in every place they traveled. Angela looked around. They didn't need another dust-collector to take home. After the store grew too crowded, Angela stepped outside, where a roving photographer approached her.

"No thank you."

The photographer took her picture anyway, and gave her a stub with a number on it. "Your picture will be ready in ten minutes," and he pointed to the booth a few feet away.

"How do you do it so fast?"

He responded something in Portuguese, which Angela didn't understand. So she strolled over to see what the partner was doing. Photos were coming off the color printer at the same time as the photographer snapped them.

"How cool is that?" Angela still refused to buy one. They had enough photos snapped every time they blinked on the cruise ship.

The clouds were starting to move away from the mountain bringing the statue into full sunlight, so Angela went to take more pictures of the view. When she saw Bodine coming out of the shop, she said "Hey Bodine. You should see how they print photos as fast as they can snap them."

"They must have Bluetooth or something. Look, we need to start back to the bus."

"I didn't see QTEE. Let me take another look around."

"I'll go hold your seat. Make sure you don't get left up here."

"Five minutes."

Angela went to the coffee shop and looked around. She didn't spot anyone who was not wearing a numbered sticker from one of the buses. She tried the gift shop again, and one last look up the steps to the statue.

As Angela turned around, the roving photographer planted himself behind her with a photo in hand. "See I told you, ten minutes."

Angela laughed as he forced the photo on her. "I said I didn't want one."

"You can pay my partner over there," he said, as he escaped.

Angela went to the printing booth to return the photo. As she left, there she spotted it, tacked onto the support beams for the booth, a manila envelope with her name, "For Angela Beaudoin."

"That's my name. This is for me." Angela whipped out her passport from her travel belt. The man in charge of the printer handed her the envelope. She looked inside and rushed off to join Bodine at the bus.

Lucky for Angela, a cable car was ready to leave for the trip down the mountain or she might have missed the bus. Bodine and the tour guide were standing outside when Angela arrived. She was fifteen minutes late. If Bodine had not been holding the bus, the group might have left her. Bodine frowned, but he knew it had to be something about QTEE.

"Well, did she show up?"

Angela apologized to the guide and to the people on the bus as she got in. It was all she could do to keep from breaking out into a big smile. When she and Bodine arrived at the last seats on the back of the bus, Angela pulled the photo out from the manila envelope. It was QTEE standing in front of the Christ the Redeemer, with a man.

Bodine had to laugh, "So you talked to her."

"No, she wasn't there, but she left the photo for me. Like she said, I would see her."

"Who is the guy with her?"

"I think it's Paulo. I don't know his whole name, but he's the one on Blaq-Kawfee from Brazil."

"Now what?"

"I'll try to call her when we get to a place where I can talk."

The tour included a few quick stops at the beautiful beaches of Rio, tour of the business section of the city and on to a Churrascaria, a Brazilian steak house. They had made up the lost time, and the restaurant had prepared to serve the group when they walked in the door. They had their fill of steak, chicken, sausages served from long skewers, and vegetables and dessert from the buffet. Since the tour guide had not yet given a time to leave, Angela took the opportunity to go outside and call QTEE.

She answered, "Hello Beautiful."

"Girl. You and Paulo?"

"Cute, isn't he?"

"But seriously, Laura, have you told anybody at home? Carlton is worried about you, and he's short on funds."

"That boy will be fine. But OK I'll call him," Laura said.

"So are you going to...stay here? How did you manage to get a Brazilian Visa anyway? We had to get a Visa way in advance just for two cruise stops."

"Paulo has connections. Angela, girl, I haven't felt so young since I was in the service."

"Good sex, huh?"

"I don't know if I can keep up. He's wearing me out. I've gotten so sore I had to make him stop."

"I don't like the sound of that," Angela said. "You make him use a condom?"

"After we got tested, we stopped using them."

"Did you see his test results?'

"Of course," Laura said.

"Look, I don't mean to be all in your business, and I know you said you speak Portuguese, but how do you say Chlamydia in Portuguese. How about Herpes?"

There was silence on the other end.

"QTEE, you still there?"

"Yes," was all Laura would say.

"Look. I need to get off this phone. The international roaming rate with the discount is like $1.50 per minute. Email me please.

We have an internet café on the ship. I'm worried about you."

"Listen, Angela," Laura said. "I guess I need to come down from my cloud and handle my business. I'll email you."

When Angela got back to the table inside, the guide waited for the women still in the restroom. The guide didn't want to call the bus driver to come on to the entrance until all her passengers were ready to board.

Bodine waited until they were on the bus to ask, "Is she OK?"

"I don't know. She said she would call Carlton to let him know she's alive. But I'm not sure about Paulo."

"He wouldn't hurt her, would he?"

"Not the way you mean. But they're having unprotected sex."

Bodine winced and turned to the window to take more photos of the city highlights.

Four hours earlier in Rio

A dozen or more tourist buses had arrived already with passengers from the cruise ship in the harbor. A black Lexus sedan waited with the motor running, beside the sign "For Buses Only" in Portuguese. The tinted windows concealed the face of the driver. A woman arrived, wearing jeans and a blouse, dark glasses covering her eyes. The driver of the sedan opened the door from the inside, leaning across the front seat. They spoke in Portuguese.

Paulo said, "What took you so long?"

Laura said, "I had to catch the tram up to the top of the mountain, leave the envelope and wait for the tram coming back.

What's your big hurry?"

"I told you I have a meeting with the family this morning, so I don't have time to meet your friend. You'll have to come with me to the meeting, and wait in the car."

Laura removed her sunglasses, flipped down the sun visor and looked at her face in the vanity mirror. Her swollen left eye had begun to turn purple. She wasn't going to cry. She would wait for her opportunity to get away. Paulo drove in silence for the next thirty minutes, and parked in front of a twenty-story glass and steel building, with the address number 1200 above the front door. He lowered the front windows a few inches, shut off the ignition and took the keys with him, as he left her in silence. Laura had only her cell phone with her, and had not an inkling of where she was. This was not the time to run away. She would plan her getaway and wait for the right time to leave. How had she trusted a man she had never met in person? Now she feared for her life.

Her cell phone rang, shaking her out of her stupor. It was Angela. This was not the time to tell her. Laura answered, "Hello Beautiful."

Las Vegas Rehab facility

At mid-morning, the sun was shining in Jackson's room. Bonita walked in, ready to take him to her house.

"I know you're ready to get out of here and get back to Memphis. They told me you would be ready this morning," she said.

Jackson looked at her with a scowl. "I appreciate all your help, but I called Carlton. He said he would come this afternoon to get me. It took me days before I could talk. I don't think I'll look at a bowl of gumbo ever again."

"I told you I misunderstood. I thought you were asking about shells. I took all the shells out."

"Yeah, anyway. I'm glad you got me to the ER, came to visit me and all, but Carlton said he would help me get my strength back so I can go home. Besides I need to talk with him about things."

"If you're sure you don't need anything from me, you have your wallet and suitcase," Bonita said. "The hotel was kind enough to take a day off your bill and check you out since you were in the hospital. The car rental wasn't as nice...I'll be going then. You have my number if you need anything. I hope we can stay in touch." She kissed Jackson on the cheek, turned on her heel and left.

By noon, Jackson was dressed and ready for Carlton to arrive. He was sitting in the chair in his room when Carlton walked in with Keisha and the baby.

Jackson stood and hugged them all, so relieved to be getting out of there.

Carlton was about to burst with his news, "I heard from Mom this morning."

Jackson, bemused, asked, "What? Where is she?"

"She didn't say. She just said she had some business to take care of, and she would be home in a few days. She transferred some money to my bank account, too."

Jackson said, "I guess you're glad she did."

"See, I was trying to keep the condo up, pay the utilities, association dues and all, and it was getting to be a stretch for me. You know she was mad at me for telling people she was dead."

"How did she know you said it?" Jackson asked.

"Ms. Angela told her."

Now Jackson was puzzled. "I haven't heard a word from Angela since I first got here in Las Vegas. Oh, I remember, she was supposed to be on a cruise, and my phone has been off. I guess I have a lot of catching up to do."

Carlton said, "Let's get out of here. We can go get some dinner, then you can rest at our house for as long as you need."

Jackson enjoyed the company of Carlton and his family. He had been confined for a couple of weeks, and had eaten only hospital food since the famous gumbo. When Laura had cut him off, he had missed the feeling of family. Jackson had a son back in North Carolina, but they talked only occasionally. It was going to be good to get his strength back in the company of young folks.

Keisha wanted to get down to the real story of Laura; Carlton wasn't telling much and Jackson didn't seem to know what happened.

"Jackson, I told Carlton he should have called Mom when he first got the note saying she was gone," she said.

Carlton said, "I didn't know where to call her. She left her phone at the condo."

Keisha said, "You could have called Jackson."

"There's no point in going back over all the past," Jackson said. "At least now we know she's coming home. How did she sound? She didn't give any clue as to where she is?"

Carlton said, "No Sir. Even the Caller ID wasn't any help. It said out of area. But, she sounded tired and worried. I'll feel so much better when she gets home."

"You and me both," said Jackson. "Did you tell her I was here?"

"I did. She seemed surprised. Do you think it would be good for you to stay here in Vegas until she gets back?"

"Naw, man. I don't know if she even wants to talk to me. I'll be on my way when I can get a flight back to Memphis."

Keisha said, "No need to rush yourself. Besides, it's nice having you with us. It feels like the circle is almost complete."

"We'll have to see what Laura has to say about it." Jackson chuckled at the thought of it.

Last Stop - Sao Paulo

Getting home from a cruise was difficult. Angela and Bodine had to pack for their departure after the tour in Rio and have their bags out in the corridor by two a.m. When they woke up the next morning, the ship was parked at the port. Bodine was the first to be dressed to watch the activity on the pier from the balcony of their cabin. All the back loaders moved the thousands of pieces of luggage from the ship to the holding area where passengers would claim their luggage before going through customs.

Angela and Bodine had a continental breakfast in the departure lounge set up for Diamond level Crown & Anchor passengers. Angela prepared for the wait to get off the ship; she had her book to read in case there was a delay. She hated it when there was finger pointing between customs and ship processing. At this juncture they didn't care who caused the delay. All they wanted was to be on their way.

Since their flight home was in the afternoon, they had scheduled a city tour. Their tour bus met them at the pier after they went through customs, and would take them to the airport at the end of the tour. The bus ride through Sao Paulo was anticlimactic after all the attractions they had already seen. More colorful hillside slums, more churches, more graffiti, and another Churrascaria for lunch where they had another round of beef, chicken and pork.

"These people must have some serious cholesterol issues," Angela said.

By the time they were checked in at the airport and had gone through security, Angela and Bodine both sighed with relief at finishing another race, and were content to find a couple of seats to lean against each other for a little snooze before they boarded their flight. Angela considered calling Laura again, but dozed off before she could get her phone out.

Angela and Bodine had a two-hour layover to change flights at Dallas-Fort Worth. They walked to the other concourse rather than take the Sky-Link because they needed to get the blood circulating in their legs again. After they located the gate, they bought something to eat since it was already after eight p.m. Bodine went and found one of the "free" internet terminals so he could get online. He liked to keep up with Yahoo Answers where he was the top answerer of travel and cruise questions. Angela turned on her phone with the intention of checking voicemail at home. Before she could make a call, her cell phone beeped with two messages. One from Jackson asking her to call him, and another from QTEE saying she would call again later. Angela was too tired to think about talking to anybody, and instead checked her messages on their home answering machine.

There were a few calls from friends and family who said in their message they didn't know if Angela was on another cruise. In addition, there was a call from Rev. Carolyn saying Isaiah, her "Little Man" had passed away. The funeral would be on Monday. Angela would have a day to unwind from the trip and still be able to go to the funeral. She reflected for a few minutes on Isaiah. He was such a gentle man. She never knew how he contracted AIDS, and didn't much care.

Bodine came back to where Angela sat to report Blaq-Kawfee was gone. "One of those bogus web pages came up. You know the ones with the Blaq-Kawfee name but links to assorted junk. The domain name is parked but there is no server for it."

American Consulate in Rio de Janeiro

"Ms. Murchison, my name is Henry Ogleby, what can we do for you?"

"I need help getting home," Laura said. "My purse was stolen with all my identification and credit cards. Before I left the States, I made a copy of my travel documents and the contents of my wallet, and it's on this memory card."

"Did you report it to the police?"

"No, I came here first."

"Where are you staying?" Mr. Ogleby asked.

"That's another problem. I just got here from Sao Paulo and I don't have a hotel."

"Where is your luggage?"

By this time, Laura started to cry. She dabbed at her eyes under her sunglasses. She knew she couldn't keep up the lie. "It's complicated."

The consulate officer had seen all kinds of weary American travelers before, and they had stories of adventure and danger. Many were young people who thought they could hitchhike their way through South America but then ran out of money and didn't have the right visa. Laura Murchison was a different case. Mr. Ogleby moved from behind his desk and sat in the chair next to her.

"Would you like to start from the beginning?" he said.

Laura spilled it all, how she had come to Brazil to see a younger man she knew from the internet. At first he was kind and attentive, but he changed and became controlling. He wouldn't let her out of his sight, and he took her passport and wallet. She had slipped out and walked to the consulate while Paulo was still sleep.

Ogleby asked, "What is the man's name and where does he live?

"I'm afraid to tell," Laura said. "His family has connections, and if he knew I came here, he would have somebody hurt me, or at least stop me from leaving. He has my credit cards, but I have all the information on this memory card, so I can get money...and I need to get my passport...I don't know where to start."

"OK, let me say this. We can help you, but it will take a few days to get the documents you need to get home. I'm going to get my assistant Ms. Locklear to take care of you, get copies of your documents from the card, get you a place to stay, notify the credit card companies, and so on. She'll help you get some clothing and toiletries so you'll be comfortable for the rest of your time here in Rio. Please stop crying."

Laura was relieved, but she couldn't stop crying. What a fool she had been. At least she had talked to Carlton. Carlton told her Jackson had gone to Las Vegas to find her. And to think she had called Jackson controlling. She didn't know what control was until she was locked in her room without the things she needed to get away.

Lord, help me get away from this place and back home.

Laura lived the good life from the time she met her first husband, Taggart, an Army doctor. Laura was a nurse, reaching the rank of colonel in the army. Taggart was controlling, too, but never like Paulo. Their marriage had suffered the same as many military couples. She would be deployed in one place while he was on the other side of the world. Laura spent so much of her marriage away from her husband, often it was just Carlton and her. She may as well have been a single mother. She could take care of herself without a man around. When Taggart was around, he wanted to be "in charge" at home like he was at work. They never could adjust to being together. When they split it was on good terms. He paid child support and alimony. However, he was never in Carlton's life. He visited during the first year, and then all they heard from him were his checks, on time every month. After he died, the monthly check to Laura continued from a trust he had created. Taggart had also instructed the trust administrator to send Laura roses every year on her birthday.

When Ms. Locklear came in, she interrupted Laura's reverie. "Ms. Murchison, we're going to start with getting you a replacement passport. We can take your photograph here, and get the process started. You should have your new documents in two days. Next, we'll go to the American Express office. Since you're a Gold Card holder, they will cancel your old account number and issue you a new card. We can get you checked in at the Windsor Hotel near here. Is that satisfactory?"

Laura said, "Oh my yes."

"I can do some shopping for you, or I can take you. Which would you prefer?"

"As much as I love to shop, I think I would be safer staying inside until I can get out of Rio. Ms. Locklear, do you usually do this kind of thing for stranded travelers?"

"No we never get this involved in a case such as yours. Your story touched Mr. Ogleby, and he said you looked so much like his sister back in the States. He hasn't seen her in several years, and the thought of her being stranded broke his heart. Besides, I'm using your American Express Gold Card services to handle as much as possible. They reserved the room at the Windsor for you, and they have someone already making calls for your clothing and personal items, to be delivered to your hotel. If anything doesn't suit you, they will return it. They will call me by the end of day with flight information for you as well. You won't have to set foot outside until you are on your way to the airport with a driver arranged by American Express."

Laura started crying again. "You have to forgive me. I'm not usually such a basket case. I'm usually the one in charge. I'm not used to having someone take care of me. Could you also get me some makeup to hide the bruises on my face before I get that passport photo?"

"Of course, you poor dear. And I made another note here," Ms. Locklear said, "Your memory card also has a list of medications. Is the list up-to-date? Do you need to get those medications today?"

"I was going to pretend I didn't need them," Laura said, "but I guess I do need them. My doctor in New York fussed at me before about going off without my meds."

CHAPTER EIGHT

Back in Raleigh, Sunday Night

It was after midnight when the weary travelers claimed their luggage and got a cab home from the airport. Even with only a two-hour time difference, they were still jet-lagged from taking naps at odd times during their trip home. Bone tired, but wide-awake, Bodine turned on his PC and dumped out the dirty clothes from his luggage. Angela couldn't let him get ahead of her in catching up on the internet, and turned her PC on, too. When she remembered the funeral for Isaiah would be at noon, she found something from her closet to set out to wear to the funeral, showered, shampooed, and crawled into bed with wet hair.

When Angela woke on Monday morning, she could smell the bacon Bodine had already cooked. Her regular breakfast was a bowl of oatmeal and green tea, but Bodine knew her weak spot for bacon, anytime. She put rollers in her damp hair, enough to get the natural curl going all in the same direction, and went downstairs to join Bodine. He already had his list to pick up the mail from the PO Box, buy a few things from the grocery store and retrieve Dusty from his sitter.

Angela's dream from the night before came back to her. She dreamed she had seen QTEE and Jackson together at Isaiah's funeral. She dismissed any thoughts of foreboding and decided the dream was merely a subconscious reminder to prepare for the funeral.

Bodine kissed her goodbye as he started out the door. "I might not be back before you leave for the funeral. How about some steaks to grill for dinner?"

Angela gave him a pained look. "How about some salmon? I don't think I've digested all the beef we ate in Brazil yet." Bodine gave her another kiss and continued out the door.

Angela sorted the pile of dirty clothes and put in the first load of wash. She threw the rest in the guest bedroom to be out of the way of Dusty when he came back. Dusty liked nesting in a pile of clothes if he found them on the floor.

Since she still had a couple of hours before she needed to leave for the funeral, she decided to call Jackson. She had a lot to catch up with him.

"Jackson, we're back home. How are you doing? It's been a busy two weeks for us. Where the heck are you?"

"I just got back home myself. I had a long visit in Las Vegas."

"Really?" Angela said. "The last I talked to you, you were going to see Bonita."

"Bonita turned out to be trouble with a capital T." Jackson told her about his time in the hospital.

"My Lord, Jackson. Are you OK now?" Angela asked.

"It wasn't all bad. I got a chance to visit with Carlton and his family. He told me he heard from Laura."

"Did she say where she was?"

"No, but she said she was coming home after she takes care of some business. You talked to her, didn't you?"

"I did." Angela said.

"And you're not going to tell me anything. Are you?"

"You know I don't tell anybody's secrets. I guess it's why people tell me all their business. They know their secrets are safe with me. I didn't tell Laura where you were either."

"Carlton told her I was in Vegas, and she seemed surprised."

"What are your plans now?" Angela asked.

"I don't know. Carlton and Keisha welcomed me into their home and they seemed to want me to get back with Laura."

"Is it what you want?"

"Remember she was the one who dumped me," Jackson said.

"You wouldn't have gone off to Vegas to find her if you didn't still love her."

"I don't think I can take being rejected again," he said.

"Here's what I think." Angela said. "The website is gone, so all those other people in her life won't be a factor in your relationship anymore. I think you should try to start over as if you never knew each other before. To tell the truth, you two had so little face time,

I don't think you ever knew each other well enough to talk about getting married."

"Angela, you know I love that woman. It's her spirit, her feisty attitude I fell for."

"But you couldn't tell me if she was diabetic or not."

"Why is that a big deal?" Jackson asked.

"I have to tell you, when Bodine and I got together, we had both been widowed. You know, when I married the first time, and said, till death us do part, I wasn't thinking somebody would die. So Bodine and I faced facts. We laid all our medical history out on the table. Somebody is going to die. If we're lucky, we may have twenty good years, but as we get older one or both of us will have something major happen. Neither one of you is a spring chicken either, so you have to face the fact Laura takes a bunch of medicine, and I bet you do, too."

"But Angela, it also means we don't have a lot of time to be wasting either."

"No, I'm not saying you should go slow. Just try to get some face time before you allow other people to make you get all insecure," Angela said.

"All right, I'll give it some thought," he said. "Do you know where she is?"

"I had a message from her when I turned my phone on yesterday in DFW airport, right after I got your message. I called you. She said she would call me back."

"Do you think I should go back to Vegas and wait for her?"

"Oh no," Angela said. "Wait until she contacts you. You said Carlton wants you two to get together? Let him set the stage for you. I'll put in a good word for you, too."

"Do you think she was seeing another man?"

"Now there you go asking me to tell secrets," she said.

"And you won't tell her about Bonita either, will you?"

"I sure won't. But you might need to tell Carlton to keep quiet." Angela laughed. "By the way, give me Carlton's phone number; I may have to call him."

After Jackson gave Angela the number, she hurried to get off the phone. "Look, let me go. I have a pile of dirty laundry, and I have to get dressed for a funeral."

"Not a family member, I hope."

"No, someone I used to help out."

"OK. Thanks for your advice. I'll give it a lot of thought," Jackson said. "Would you let me know when Laura gets back?"

"I sure will, but Carlton may beat me to it."

During the call, Angela had a call waiting notice she ignored. When she hung up with Jackson, she saw an "Out of Area" on the Caller ID. She wondered if it might have been Laura.

Angela had checked her main email account while they were on the cruise, but only read the ones from family or that looked urgent. Now there were a few dozen messages she needed to answer. Her other email accounts could wait another day. And there was no avoiding Facebook, even if it did waste the hours away. She read all her messages and scanned through the notifications. With so many more people on her friends list than she'd had on Blaq-Kawfee, it was no wonder another hour passed before she noticed the time.

It's a good thing Angela had picked out something last night to wear to the funeral because the time had slipped by and she feared she would be late. When she reached the funeral home, there were several clusters of people milling about in the parking lot and at the front entrance. She realized she didn't know Isaiah's last name. It was the practice of the AIDS ministry to establish boundaries and allow the care partners to decide if they would give out last names. Isaiah knew her only as Ms. Angela.

There were at least three deceased prepared for viewing or a funeral, so Angela wandered down the main hall where she could read the names by the doors until she found Isaiah Jenkins. The service had not started yet, so she slipped into the back row. She recognized a couple of people from the transportation team and nodded toward them. When she saw Isaiah's daughter Delicia, on the front row, she went to express condolences. The casket was closed, but a large photograph of Isaiah in an army uniform was displayed on an easel. He was much younger and healthy looking. Angela could only wonder how his life had come to this end.

Delicia's minister read scripture and spoke about Delicia's love for her daddy. The minister had never met Isaiah, but he was there to support Isaiah's daughter. The single soloist was a woman who was at least six feet tall, and must have weighed three-hundred pounds. She sang "His Eye is on the Sparrow." Her powerful voice filled the room, spilled out into the hallway, and even the people in the parking lot could feel the spirit. Angela feared she would embarrass herself by crying, but when the song ended, everyone in the room had reached for tissues. Angela slipped out the back door as quickly as she could and rushed to inhale the fresh air.

If the preacher didn't preach Isaiah into heaven, surely the singer sang him there.

Angela heard the comments in the parking lot as she reached her car. "That Brenda can shonuff sing."

Rio de Janeiro International Airport

Laura made it through customs and security with her one piece of luggage containing the few clothes Ms. Locklear had gotten for her short stay at the Windsor Hotel. She found her departure gate and sighed she would soon be back on US soil. Ms. Locklear had laughed at her disguise of dark glasses and a big hat, convincing Laura it would draw more attention than a simple outfit of jeans and a neutral colored jacket. She was away from Paulo for good.

Laura settled into a seat to wait for boarding and attempted to call Angela again. Again there was no answer, but she didn't leave a message. She would have the seven-hour flight to sort out how badly she had messed up her life. She could hear Angela's voice ringing in her ears, "How about Herpes?" She would see her good doctor again in New York before flying on to Las Vegas. Dr. Karnic never looked at her with judging eyes. If she had some incurable disease, she would do what she had to do.

"There's no fool like an old fool," she told herself.

Days later

Angela and Bodine were back into their routine at home, with Facebook as Angela's main online waste of time. Bodine had to catch up with his answers to travel questions on Yahoo. Dusty was happy to be back home where he could sit on Bodine's lap and look at the computer screen. They still had not heard from Laura. Angela had called the last number she had, but it went straight to voicemail. She had left a message one time. Many of her friends from Blaq-Kawfee were now on Facebook, but nobody was saying anything about Laura. If there had been any chatter about Laura in the last two weeks, Angela couldn't find it.

She called Harman.

"Hi, Harman. We got back a few days ago, and I thought I would check to see if you've heard from Laura."

"Hey Angela. As a matter of fact, she called me yesterday and left a message. She's back in New York. I tried calling back and didn't get an answer. Didn't you talk to her while you were gone?"

"I talked to her briefly, but she didn't tell me she was coming back."

Harman said, "I signed up for Facebook, but the old vibe from Blaq-Kawfee isn't there. I found a few friends, and said hello, but it's like Laura disappeared and nobody noticed."

"I'm feeling it, too. I need to find out where Laura is. I didn't want to call Carlton, but I guess I should," Angela said.

"Let me know what you hear," Harman said.

"I sure will, Harman."

Angela tried to wait before calling Carlton, hoping Laura might call first. She didn't want to have to answer any questions about where Laura might be. And to think she had accused Carlton of being evasive.

It was evening when Angela couldn't stand to wait any longer so she called.

"Hi Carlton, it's me Angela. I'm just touching bases to see if you've heard anything from your mom."

"Hi Ms. Angela. She called me this morning from New York. She said she was tired of traveling and she would be home in a few days. She said she was visiting friends in New York."

"I'm glad to hear it. Did she sound all right?" Angela asked.

"She sounded tired. She asked about Keisha and the baby, and I put the baby on the phone for a minute. He listened to her voice and smiled. Haven't you heard anything from her?"

"We've been away on a cruise, and I tried calling her when we got back and left a message. I was hoping she was back in Las Vegas. If you hear from her again, let her know I asked about her."

"I sure will, Ms. Angela."

After Angela hung up, the doorbell rang downstairs. Angela looked out the front window and saw the motion-detector lights had come on in front of the house. There was a car in the driveway, a red Corvette. Bodine was half undressed getting ready to turn in early.

"Bodine, are you expecting anybody?"

"Do I look like I'm ready for company?"

"Who do we know with a Corvette?" Angela asked.

They looked at each other in a shared light bulb moment and said in unison, "QTEE."

CHAPTER NINE

Late Night Visitor

Angela ran downstairs to open the door. Laura had never, ever paid them a visit.

"Girl," Angela said, "what in the world? If I knew you were coming, I'd have baked a cake. Come in."

Angela and Laura hugged and laughed. Bodine stayed upstairs, knowing he didn't want to be in on their conversation. Angela took Laura into the kitchen where they wouldn't disturb Bodine. Dusty was in his crate in the corner of the kitchen. He lifted his head and settled back down to sleep.

Angela had so many questions. "You'll have to spend the night with us. Now tell me everything. First, where did you get the car? I thought you left your Corvette in Vegas."

Laura smiled one of her secret smiles. "It's a rental. It's a few years newer than my car back home. I decided I could use the drive time to collect myself before I go home. Whatchu got to eat?"

Angela pulled out some leftover chicken and vegetables and microwaved a plate of food for Laura. When Laura opened a pack of cigarettes, Angela stopped her.

"We don't smoke, and I don't even own an ashtray. If you want to smoke, you'll have to go outside or to the garage."

Laura wrinkled her face, and said, "I'll wait." Then she settled down to eat while Angela had a cup of yogurt.

"You're looking all brown and healthy," Angela said. "What would you like to drink?"

"You know I want coffee...black. And I did get a lot of time in the sun."

"Are you planning to drink coffee so you can drive all night? I'm serious about your staying with us." Angela set up the coffeemaker to brew a pot of coffee.

"Thanks for the hospitality. I didn't want to impose. I didn't plan where I was going next."

"We have plenty room. Besides, we need to talk. What happened in Rio?"

"I guess that's why I came here before going home," Laura said. "I don't know what I'm going to do. After we talked on the phone in Rio, I started thinking about STDs and all, and I confronted Paulo about what he might have given me. He turned on me. He went from sweet to mean and controlling. I had to sneak out of the house while he was sleep and get help from the US Consulate to get out of Rio."

Laura didn't want to tell Angela how Paulo had hit her before that day. He became angry again when she wanted to meet Angela at the Christ the Redeemer statue. If she had left the first time he hit her, she could have left with her own things and some of her dignity still intact. When she stayed, it had only gotten worse. She couldn't tell anybody how stupid she had been.

"NOOOO. I'm so sorry," Angela said, leaning across the table to hug her friend. "I'm glad you're here and safe. I didn't mean to get all in your business. It just hit me something was really wrong."

"It pissed me off when you brought it up," Laura admitted, "but after I got to thinking, I knew it too. When I got back to New York, I went to my doctor again, and got tested. Sure enough Herpes. He prescribed some antiviral medicine I'm supposed to take at the first sign of an outbreak. I was so stunned about having Herpes it didn't sink in until I was on I-95, coming south. I'm supposed to wait until I have an outbreak before I do something about it. It would mess up my sex life, if I had a sex life. And I can forget about having any kind of relationship in the future."

"You sound like one of our Blaq-Kawfee friends a few years ago."

"Who?"

"She swore me to secrecy. Besides, you know I don't tell secrets."

"Yeah, Sister Angela's confessions. But can you tell me what happened."

"This particular BK woman dated a man she met online,"

Angela began. "They got tested; he showed her his test results and all. They were both disease-free. They dated about a year before they started getting on each other's nerves. They broke up, and she was fine with it. But she started noticing what she thought was a recurring yeast infection every few months. She tried some over-the-counter cream she thought helped, but it kept coming back. It got consistently worse. She finally got a magnifying mirror to check it out. She looked on the internet for photos of something looking like the rash she had. By the time she called me about it, she was in a real state...crying and cursing the man. He was the only man she had been with in over five years, so it had to've been him."

"So what did she want you to do?" Laura asked.

"I guess she needed a shoulder to cry on, but I convinced her to get tested again. She didn't want to go to her regular doctor. Didn't want him to look at her differently. I suggested she go to a clinic. We got online and looked for a clinic near her. I convinced her those people see so many different ailments they wouldn't care who she was."

"Then what?"

"She didn't call me back for a couple of weeks," Angela said. "We were online doing our usual hellos, but not saying anything. I finally called her. She started crying when she heard my voice. It was Herpes. The clinic gave her a prescription for an antiviral to take at the first sign of an outbreak...just like you. She cursed the clinic and the guy, and cried about her life being over. I listened. I told her there had to be a better way to deal with this thing. We both got online and searched for Herpes cures. There were pages and pages of links to all kinds of websites. Lots of natural cures. Many religious folks talking about abstinence. Even some people taking silver to cure their Herpes."

"Silver? Does it work?" Laura asked.

"I saw a guest on a talk show a few weeks ago who claimed silver cured his Herpes. But it turned his skin blue." Angela started laughing thinking about it.

"What? Blue like Smurfs? That's not funny," Laura said.

"No, not a cartoon color blue. More like pale with a blue tinge. Like a vampire."

"What did our nameless friend do?" Laura asked.

"She found a forum site for people with Herpes. She told me the name, but I forget."

"Did they help?"

"I didn't talk to her again for over a month, but when she did call, she thanked me. She said she had made friends with people on the forum. There were a lot of teenagers on there who couldn't tell their parents and were talking suicide. She talked to a lot of them online, and helped them see all was not lost. Helping them did more for her than she expected. She said there was a group of silver people on there. Nobody criticized anybody else. Then she started talking to the forum leaders who posted information about the medication they were taking. They use a generic antiviral they take daily. They don't wait for an outbreak. Some of them claim they haven't had an outbreak in years. They say it's not a cure because the virus is still there without symptoms."

"So I could control the virus and be symptom free?" Laura asked.

"That's what they say."

"Why didn't my doctor tell me this? I could have my life back."

"You have to ask him," Angela said. "Some doctors don't seem to take Herpes seriously. It's not fatal, and a large percentage of the population has it if you count cold sores."

"OK, enough of that subject, Sister Confessor. I saw the website is gone. Do you think I should get it back?"

"In the time you've been gone, the BK folks have moved on. They have a little BK group on Facebook where Lester can call people names and nobody will have him banned."

"They don't even miss me?"

"They miss you," Angela lied. "Everyday somebody mentions your name and wishes you were there."

"Is Jackson there?"

"I haven't seen him. It's like he doesn't have any interest in being online if you're not there."

"Carlton told me he came to Vegas to find out how I died."

"That was something." Angela said.

"Do you think he still loves me?" Laura asked.

"I don't know if I should get in the middle of this. You dumped him, didn't you?"

"I didn't know what I wanted. I just needed to get away. After the thing with Paulo, I realized...I don't know. I suppose I would have to tell him about Paulo, huh?" Laura asked.

"If you want to have a relationship with Jackson, you would have to tell him about the Herpes."

Laura's mouth formed a small circle as she said, "Oh."

Angela's head started to nod. It was only eleven p.m., but the conversation was exhausting. She said, "Let's call it a night. We could both use some rest. We'll talk in the morning."

Morning Kawfee

Angela woke up to the smell of coffee and bacon. Bodine loved to cook, and he didn't mind sabotaging Angela's diet. He would say, "Nobody is making you eat it." Angela hit the shower and dressed. She knew Laura would make a willing conspirator for Bodine.

The kitchen showed the leftovers of coffee, bacon and eggs, sliced tomatoes, and biscuits. Angela poured herself a cup and watched the two outside surveying Bodine's garden. He didn't mind talking about gardening, his next best thing to do after traveling. While they were traveling, there wasn't much rain, and now Bodine hoped to salvage his tomato and pepper plants with extra mulching from the compost pile. Laura walked through the rows with him, sipping on her cup of coffee. When Angela joined them, Laura gave her a wink. Dusty was right on Angela's heels as she walked across the backyard. After they had put up an invisible fence around the garden, he learned to stay out of Bodine's space back there.

When Bodine was out of earshot, Laura whispered, "Weakest cup of coffee I ever had."

Angela contained her laughter. Bodine always said Angela's coffee was strong enough to walk. Angela pointed Laura to the gazebo, where the two of them went to continue their conversation from the night before.

Before Angela could say anything, Laura pulled out her cigarettes, and the soap dish she had brought from the guest bathroom to use as an ashtray. Angela didn't stop her from smoking, but twitched her nose and shook her head.

Laura admired the garden and back yard, "I love the space you have back here. You can't tell from the street that you have such a large yard. And the woods behind you give you a lot of privacy."

"Thanks," Angela said. "Bodine is more of an outdoor person than I am, but I do like sitting on the deck in the summertime. We expect those woods will be cut down for another development before long." Then Angela broke into a big smile before beginning, "You won't believe the dream I had last night."

"Was I in it?"

"You and I were in a limo in Las Vegas. You were all decked out in your wedding gown and veil."

"What? You lie," Laura said.

"No, really. I was your bridesmaid. The limo pulled up to one of those chintzy wedding chapels, and we got out. I took you to a room in the back, and went looking for the groom."

"Who was the groom?"

"Don't interrupt." Angela said. "There were several men standing at the altar, and the only one I recognized was Bodine. I don't know who you were supposed to be marrying. That was when the smell of bacon woke me up. I was going to ask you did you have any revelations while you slept last night."

"You mean about Jackson? I thought you had it all wrapped up in your dream."

"About anything," Angela said. Then she rattled off her list of Laura's issues, "Jackson, the website, driving to Vegas by yourself, living with Herpes."

"Damn, woman, you sure know how to get straight to the point. I decided to do it this way. I'll call Jackson, and try to feel out what he might be thinking. If it sounds positive, I'll make Memphis my next stop. I might even ask him to make the drive with me to Vegas."

"Ooh, that sounds good to me," Angela said.

"As for the rest of it, the website dragged me down. I can use the money for something else, like replacing all the clothes I had to leave in Rio."

"Tell me how did it work out? You had to leave with nothing?" Angela asked.

"Paulo went ballistic. He started cursing at me...I didn't know what the hell he was saying in Portuguese but I knew it was nasty. Then he started pushing me around. I hid in the bathroom for the rest of the day. After he went to sleep, I couldn't get to my luggage without waking him. So at first light, I got out of there with a small purse and my phone. I remembered after I got out that I didn't have my wallet or my passport because Paulo had taken them.

Laura continued, "I have never had a man to put his hands on me in such a way. I wasn't going to hang around and let him hit me. You know Jackson would never lay a hand on me. My late husband Taggart, even with all we went through, never put his hands on me. And there was the handsome Mr. Ogleby at the Consulate. He certainly eased my mind."

Laura told how the nice man at the American Consulate had helped her get her passport replaced and clothes to wear until she could get a flight to New York.

"Have you eaten anything yet?" Angela asked. "I saw all the food Bo made."

"I had his weak coffee. I don't eat much breakfast anyway."

"Sit with me while I have my oatmeal. And I can't let bacon go to waste. I'll make you a pot of real coffee," Angela said.

They went back in the house, where Laura made the coffee, and Angela made oatmeal.

"Why don't I give you the twenty-five cent tour of Raleigh?" Angela asked. "We can have lunch downtown, and later we'll take Bodine with us to dinner. We'll take you to the 42nd Street Oyster Bar."

"You don't even have a 42nd Street in Raleigh," Laura said.

"But we do have an Oyster Bar by that name," Angela said. "Why don't you give Jackson a call? He should be up by now."

Laura went into the other room, while Angela finished her oatmeal and cleaned up the kitchen.

When Laura came out, the smug smile on her face made Angela ask, "What? What did he say?"

"He said, 'It's nice to meet you, Mrs. Murchison. At least that's what Angela said I'm supposed to say.' How are you keeping my secrets but telling him what to do?" Laura asked.

"I didn't give him instructions," Angela said. "I just said you need to start over from the beginning, like you never knew each other before."

"Uh huh. I'm messing with you," Laura said. "You're right. All the old issues, all the jealousy and control issues are water under the bridge. I told him I would leave Raleigh early in the morning and be in Memphis in time for dinner. How many miles is it anyway?"

"Oh, about eight hundred. And you'd better not speed. You know radar works overtime on red sports cars."

"Yikes. With that distance, I should fly instead."

"It might be worth it to see if you can get a flight, let's look on Orbitz."

Angela took Laura upstairs to her office.

"I love your house," Laura said. "It would be nice to have a longer visit."

Laura admired Angela's collections of clocks and mirrors. "You can check out yourself all over this house." And when she saw the family photo gallery in the upstairs hallway she stopped and said,

"You have a nice looking family. I remember some of these photos you had online."

When she saw Angela's messy desk, Laura asked, "Who has the neat desk?"

Angela said, "Don't talk about my desk now. I work hard at what I do."

"And what exactly do you do?"

Angela laughed and opened up a browser on her computer, and searched on Orbitz for a flight to Memphis. "There's a flight at seven a.m. tomorrow that will get you there before ten. You have to change in Atlanta. And it's less than $300."

"I would have to turn in the rental, and check in by six a.m.? What do you think?"

"Let's do our Raleigh tour starting with finding the rental place at the airport," Angela said. "When we get back you can decide if you want to book it. The alternative would be leaving here about four a.m. to get there before dinner."

"OK, you're my guide," Laura said.

Angela told Bodine the plan for the day, and hoped he would join them for dinner at 42nd Street. Angela showed Laura how easy it was to get to the airport from her house. Within thirty minutes they had found the rental return, and were on the way downtown to start the twenty-five cent tour. Angela liked to show visitors all the colleges in Raleigh. NC State, Meredith College, Peace College, St Mary's, and not to miss the HBCU's, St. Augustine's College and Shaw University. In addition, she mentioned Wake Technical College and an assortment of for profit universities. Angela liked to tell visitors if you want a college education, you ought to be able to get one in North Carolina. Between Durham, Chapel Hill and Raleigh, you couldn't go far without bumping into a college.

They made a stop at Pullen Park and rode on the newly renovated antique carousel. Laura thought it was silly at first, two grown women on a kiddie ride. Nevertheless, when she saw parents and children enjoying the newly painted horses and chariots, she let herself enjoy the ride as much as Angela did. "Don't tell me Bodine rides this, too," she said.

"But of course."

Angela drove them on to the Farmer's Market, past the stalls of watermelons, and parked where they could smell the berries from the booths inside...strawberries, blackberries, blueberries, and tomatoes fresh off the vine. Fresh cut flowers stood in buckets of water. In the air-conditioned pavilion they sampled fresh-baked apple pie and peach cobbler, but resisted the homemade peanut brittle and barbecue sauce. When they had had their fill of samples, and strolled on to the seafood restaurant in the market to share a fried fish sandwich for lunch, Angela took it as an opportunity to ask Laura one more burning question. "What made you write that note to Carlton, 'Tell them I died'?"

Laura tried to explain. "It was something building up in me for several months. Remember last year I added a PayPal button on the bottom of the Blaq-Kawfee homepage, asking for donations? You,

Bodine, and Lester were the only ones to send me money. It wasn't like I needed the money or anything; I just thought people should share in the expense."

"At the time," Angela said, "I thought you had some bills mounting, so I suggested the calendar thing. What I had in mind was like those old women in the UK who had semi-nude photos taken with their parts concealed by a plant or piano or something. They made a lot of money for their charity selling those calendars. Then too many people got involved."

"That's when I decided to take charge of it and get a printer to give me a good price." Laura said, "After I found out how many I would have to print to get a profit, I got frustrated. Besides nobody seemed interested in buying one anyway. After that there were so many negative forum topics going around about how the site should be free. And people were calling me all the time with suggestions about advertising."

"See, that's what people are used to," Angela said. "We expect the internet to be free. Google doesn't charge a fee for searches or mail or Picasa or any of their other products. They make their big bucks from advertising. Those pennies per click add up to millions."

"That's what everybody kept telling me. I started feeling like a little fish in a big ocean where I didn't belong. So I split. That note to Carlton, I wrote it on the spur of the moment, not thinking he would tell anybody."

"I hope now you feel like you can trust your friends to have your back, so you don't have to go running off again," Angela said.

"Now you're making me cry."

They finished their fish, and dropped their litter in the receptacle before continuing on Angela's tour. They took the scenic route back to the house, so Angela could show Laura some of the neighborhoods, shopping malls, and golf course communities all over Raleigh.

Laura said, "It's no wonder so many magazines are calling Raleigh a great place to live."

Since they were in the neighborhood, Angela decided to drop by to see Maxine and Leo at their retirement home. They were happy to see Angela, and were surprised to see she brought a friend with her. Angela had planned to stay thirty minutes, but this time Maxine had lost her purse. She didn't need to carry a purse in the retirement home, but she didn't like to leave the apartment without it. They had not seen Maxine's red Liz Claiborne purse in two days. Maxine had been keeping it under the sofa where it would be handy, and she thought it would be safe from being stolen. She was sure somebody had taken it. Leo wasn't so sure it had been stolen, and had held off reporting it being gone.

Laura kept the old folks occupied with talk about Las Vegas while Angela assessed the situation. This wasn't the first time Angela had needed to search for something Maxine had lost. In her wandering and attempts at straightening up the small apartment, she often put things away in inappropriate places where nobody would look. So Angela looked through all the drawers in the kitchen and bedroom. She shifted every item on each hanger in the closet, in case Maxine had hung the purse on a hanger. Next Angela looked through all the shoeboxes and storage boxes on the shelves. She tried crawling on her knees to see what might be at a lower eye-level. When she was about to give up, she spotted the purse on the bookshelf between two books by Walter Mosley, *Little Scarlet* and *Black Betty*. Maxine was happy to see her purse. Leo decided it was a good time for him to keep the wallet. Maxine didn't have any cash in it, but it would be a major inconvenience to have to replace the insurance and Medicare cards.

By the time they left the couple, Laura and Leo were the best of friends, and Maxine wondered why anyone would want to live in Las Vegas with all those lights and people gambling. When they got back home, they found Bodine napping in the shade on the deck. Angela didn't wake him. She knew he had gotten up early and had worked hard in the yard. Dusty was sleeping at his feet, tuckered out from following Bodine from around the perimeter of the garden.

Laura said, "I could use a nap myself. I haven't gotten much sleep since I left Rio. Do you mind if I crash until dinner?"

"Go right ahead," Angela said. "I'm going to bump around on Facebook for a while. We can do your air reservation when you get up."

Angela hadn't signed on all day, and did her usual greeting friends whom she saw online. She noticed there was a Facebook message for her. It was from Paulo.

Hello, this is Paulo from BK. Have you heard from QTEE?

Angela started to delete it, but first she clicked on the name to see what information he might have on his page. She could see only the head outline they used when there was no photo. Angela deleted the message. She had been online for an hour, when Laura appeared at Angela's office door.

Angela said, "I thought you were asleep."

"I had a power nap. It's all I need. What time is dinner?"

"We'll leave here about 5:30. It won't be crowded so early."

Laura looked worried when she said, "I'm thinking I should drive to Memphis. If I turn in my car, I'll have to worry about getting home to Las Vegas. I'm not sure how things will work out with Jackson. I may have to tell him about Paulo."

"Yes, you definitely will," Angela said. "Speaking of the devil, Paulo left me a message on Facebook. He wanted to know if I had heard from you. I deleted the message."

"How did he know how to find you on Facebook?"

"Before BK shut down, a lot of us said we would be going to Facebook, and we gave our Facebook names," Angela said. "We left the country before it shut down. His message said, Paulo from BK. Is his last name Ochoa?"

"That's him."

"He has your cell phone number, doesn't he?"

"I ditched that phone," Laura said. "Remind me to give you my new number."

"It's a good thing I stopped keeping a book for phone numbers. You would have filled several pages by now."

"Yeah, I know. How am I going to tell Jackson?"

"Like I told him, treat it like it's a brand new relationship," Angela said. "Go slow. No sex until you find the right time to tell him. When you went missing, I was surprised how much he didn't know about you."

"Like what?" Laura asked.

"Your medical history," Angela said. "After Carlton told me you had left without your meds, he gave me a list of what you were taking. I had to ask Jackson if he knew you were diabetic. He didn't have a clue."

"Damn. You were all up in my business. Why should I have to tell Jackson all my ailments?"

"You were engaged. You were ready to trust a man with your life without giving him any information about your health."

"Did you and Bodine put all your medical problems out there before you got married?" Laura asked.

"We did," Angela said. "I guess it was easy for us since we had both been widowed. We were accustomed to the reality of sickness and death. Has Jackson told you about his ailments?"

"I supposed he has as many ailments as I do. He was in the hospital during the years we were talking on the phone. He had cancer. He wasn't too specific about what kind. You're right, we should have discussed it."

"Once you get started talking about diabetes, heart disease, and cancer...Herpes may seem like small potatoes." Angela had to laugh at herself for saying it.

"OK, we'll go slow. If I wait until we're on the way to Las Vegas to tell him, he'll be trapped in the car, and won't be able to run away," Laura said.

"Laura, that man loves you. He's not running anywhere. Let's get cleaned up for dinner."

"Do I have to dress up?" Laura asked.

"Raleigh has gotten like New York. People wear anything they want, except in the exclusive places with requirements for men to wear a jacket. You might see anything from jeans to tuxedos and gowns. I'll wear slacks and a top, no sneakers. Whatever you have in your suitcase will work."

CHAPTER TEN

Laura said, "You weren't kidding. The 42nd Street Oyster Bar in Raleigh. If this place were in Manhattan, they wouldn't have a parking lot, but they would have twice as many tables in this space. Otherwise, it does have a New York kind of atmosphere. What's good to eat here?" Laura took a look at all the pages of the menu.

Bodine said, "It's our favorite place to take company from out of town. I don't eat oysters, but Angela does. My favorite is the seafood platter. It might be too much food for you. And I have to warn you about the hush puppies."

Laura said, "What's wrong with the hush puppies?"

"They are so good; we might finish off the whole basket before they bring our dinner. And you'll be too full to eat your dinner."

"They are good," Angela said, "I usually have fried oysters. After I have too many hush puppies, I'll end up taking half my oysters home to eat tomorrow."

When the server returned with a basket of hushpuppies and their drink orders, they placed their orders for dinner. After Laura had eaten half the hushpuppies, Bodine grabbed the basket and divvied up the rest...One for Laura, two for me, one for Angela...and so on. A few people who knew Bodine and Angela stopped by their table to say hello. They introduced their friend Laura as their long-time internet friend. Bodine liked to watch their friends' expressions of disbelief when he introduced their internet friends.

When they got home from dinner, Laura knew she needed to get some sleep before her planned early start in the morning. She told Angela she would set her cell phone to ring and let herself out.

"You know I have to lock the door behind you. Tap on my door when you're ready, and I'll come down. I'm a light sleeper," Angela said.

Laura said OK and went off to bed.

Dusty was restless to get outside once again, so Bodine took him for a short walk down the cul-de-sac and back. Dusty seemed interested in something under Laura's car, and started barking until Bodine looked under the car. Bodine could see something furry under there, that wouldn't come out as long as Dusty barked. After Dusty allowed Bodine to take him inside to his crate, Bodine went back outside with a flashlight. There he found the neighborhood stray black cat, "Socks." Bodine could see Socks under the car with her litter of kittens.

He wouldn't have done anything to disturb the kittens, if Laura had not been planning to leave early in the morning. So he put his ingenuity to work and found a large box in which he put a large saucer of milk. Bodine couldn't tell Angela what he was doing, knowing she would envision all those cats coming to live with them. He would let Dusty chase the cats away in the morning. Meanwhile Socks and her kittens didn't mind piling into the box Bodine placed inside the fence.

Angela didn't know about Socks until Bodine and Dusty went out for their morning walk. Dusty knew the minute he bounded out the front door something had invaded his territory, and he started sniffing and barking, as Angela had never heard from him before. This time Bodine had to put Dusty back in the house while he sent Socks and her family packing. Then Angela brought Dusty out to make sure the cats would not come back.

Angela began what she hoped would be a lazy day at home, when the phone rang. It was Laura. She had made it to Knoxville TN, where she stopped for breakfast. When she was ready to go again, the car wouldn't start. She called Triple-A, who towed the car to the rental company, and she was waiting to get a replacement.

"They don't have any Corvettes," Laura said. "The only decent car they have ready is an Escalade. Can you see me in an Escalade? It's messing with my style. I called Jackson, and he doesn't think I should try to drive all the way to Memphis today. He suggested I stop for the night in Nashville and he would meet me there. I told him we wouldn't need to have two cars. But I will stop in Nashville. This layover here is making me tired."

Angela said, "I agree it's a good idea for you to stop in

Nashville. It's still a long way. And you're right, you can't be feeling the Escalade, but it's probably a smoother ride for a long distance. You can trade it for something more sporty when you get to Memphis. Give me a call when you stop for the night."

After Laura's visit, Angela was ready to burst with the news to her online friends, but she knew she needed to keep it quiet. She had already asked Bodine to keep it quiet, but she couldn't resist going online to join in the latest chatter. She did mention to a few people she had had company the day before. She liked to joke about having a Bed & Breakfast in her house since they often had family to visit for the holidays. They weren't expecting anybody until summer.

Angela remembered she hadn't talked to Harman. Since Laura had so much else on her mind, she didn't mention him to Laura. He might be another person to keep her from getting back with Jackson.

Angela thought, what am I doing? I don't mean to be playing matchmaker. Nevertheless, she did think Laura and Jackson were meant to be together. Since she had told Harman she would call him, she did.

"Harman, you will not believe who blew through here yesterday in a red Corvette."

"NOOO...why didn't you call me?"

"I'm calling you now," Angela said. "We had so much girl-talk to catch up on, and she didn't stay long."

"Is she OK? How does she look?"

"She looks great. You saw the photo I posted on BK when she was missing, didn't you? She's looking all fat and healthy. And she's had some sun, so she's glowing."

"Which way was she going when she left you?" Harman asked.

"She was driving a rental car, and had in mind to drive all the way back to Vegas. She said she was going to take her time and make stops on the way."

"Did she show up without telling you she was coming?"

"She sure did," Angela said, "late at night. I looked out and saw a red Corvette in the driveway."

"That's how QTEE rolls. I bet she has a new phone number."

"Yes she does." Angela gave Harman the number.

"I'll give her a call later in the day. I don't want her on her phone while she's driving the Corvette. She'll probably be speeding."

"You know how she rolls."

"Thanks for letting me know my girl is safe. Stay sweet, Angela."

"Bye, Harman."

Angela joined Bodine outside and told him about the call to Harman.

"You really are trying to get Laura and Jackson back together, aren't you?" Bodine asked.

"I wasn't planning to, but it seems so natural for them to be together."

"Just let nature run its course, and what will be will be." Bodine grabbed her in one of his bear hugs and kissed her.

Angela giggled, and said, "I love you, Sweetie."

Bodine said, "I wish I had thought about it earlier, but today would have been a good day for the beach. Why don't we plan it for tomorrow? It's supposed to be warm again. Do you have anything on your calendar tomorrow?"

"I don't have a thing. No appointments, no meetings, and I can skip my muscle class."

"Let's plan to leave about 9 a.m. Rush hour will be over by then," Bodine said.

When it got close to dinnertime, Angela asked as she did most days, "What do you want for dinner?"

Bodine did all the grocery shopping, so it should have been easy for Angela to pull together something from the freezer, the pantry, the refrigerator or the garden. She thought it was time for her to retire from cooking. She had cooked every day in the thirty years of her first marriage. Bodine would have been happy to eat out regularly, but Angela wanted to avoid the calories from restaurant food. After five years of marriage, they realized they had different styles of cooking. Angela cooked slim while Bodine cooked fat. Bodine liked gravy or at least some kind of sauce on most of his food. They could usually agree on fish. Fish was healthy, and they both liked it broiled in the oven. Bodine would cover his in sauce. If Angela were ever away at dinnertime, Bodine would take the opportunity to fry something. This night they would dine on broiled salmon and spinach. If Bodine didn't get enough to eat, he would make up for it with his stash of roasted peanuts.

It was their custom to settle down for the evening with some TV or reading. Angela was back online writing her blog. She often wrote book or movie reviews, or she wrote about any subject that stuck in her head. Angela expected to get a call from Laura with an update on her trip across Tennessee. Instead, she got a call from her son Aaron.

"Hey Mom, I'm at Duke Hospital with Stephen. He's got another urinary tract infection. They have him hooked up to an IV with antibiotics."

"Oh, no. How bad is he feeling this time?" Angela asked.

"I think this time he recognized the signs before it got too bad. But they want to keep him overnight to be sure. I'll stay with him until they get him a room. You want to talk to him?"

"Sure." To Stephen, Angela said, "Stephen, did you get a high fever this time?"

"No, I think it was only up to a hundred and one degrees when Aaron called me," Stephen said. "I think I could tell by the smell that I had an infection. The ER doc said he didn't know if the smell made any difference, but it seemed to have worked for me."

"I'm glad your brother is nearby so he could help you get to the ER," Angela said.

"I was going to call the emergency nursing service, but Aaron called me first," Stephen said.

Aaron was back on the phone. "Yeah, Ma, something told me to call Stephen. It hit me something might be wrong."

"I'm glad you're there to help him. Does he want me to come and check on him tonight?"

"You know Stephen, he wants to be independent," Aaron said.

Then Angela could hear Stephen in the background, "Yeah, when am I going to get a car?"

Aaron said, "See what I mean? I'll call you when they get him a room."

"Thanks, I love you. And tell Stephen I love him too."

"Love you, too, Mom, Bye."

Angela went into the bedroom to tell Bodine about Stephen.

"He'll be all right in the morning, won't he?" Bodine asked. "We may need to cancel the beach."

"We can play it by ear. I'll call Stephen in the morning to see how he's doing."

The phone rang again, announcing an out of area call. It didn't give Angela a good feeling, but she answered the phone.

"I'm trying to call Angela Platte Beaudoin. Is this Angela?"

"Yes."

"This is Paulo Ochoa from Blaq-Kawfee."

Angela didn't know how to respond, so she said, "Excuse me?"

"This is Paulo Ochoa from Brazil."

"Who are you calling?"

"I am QTEE's friend."

Angela said, "I'm sorry, you must have the wrong number," and hung up.

Bodine heard Angela's side of the conversation and concluded it was really a wrong number, but he became concerned when he saw Angela fanning herself as beads of sweat formed on her brow. "Are you all right?" he asked.

"That was Paulo from Brazil."

"How did he get this number?"

"Somehow he got my full name on Facebook. With my full name, it's easy to find me. I wonder if I'm the only Angela Platte Beaudoin on the internet."

"He may think it was a wrong number, and won't call back," Angela said.

When the phone rang again, Angela jumped.

This time Bodine grabbed the phone and answered loudly, "Hello."

Laura was on the other end, "Well HELLO to you, too, Bodine. I'm checking in. I told Angela I would call when I stopped for the night."

"Oh hi, Laura. She's right here." Bodine handed the phone to Angela.

"Hi Laura. I'm recovering from a hot flash. Are you in Nashville?"

"Hot flashes, huh? Yes, I'm checked in," Laura said. "I got something to eat and I'm in for the night. You had to give Harman my number, didn't you?"

"I figured I owed him since he was the one you called in New York and that's how I found you in Brazil."

Laura said, "So many men, so little time."

Angela said, "You don't know how not-funny that is. I had a call from Paulo. He was the cause of the hot flash."

"Oh no. He hasn't tracked me down, has he?"

"I pretended it was a wrong number. I wasn't about to acknowledge I knew what he was talking about. Does he have your number in Las Vegas?"

"He had that number," Laura said, "but how long have I been gone? Unless Carlton let them cut off the number at the condo, Paulo will be getting a response from the answering machine. I wonder what he might be thinking. I'll have to call the answering machine and see what's on it."

"It ought to be interesting," Angela said.

"Hold on Angela, I think this is Jackson calling. Let me call you back."

"Call me tomorrow. It's getting near my bedtime." Angela climbed into Bodine's recliner with him and gave him a tickle.

Early to Rise

"Not that phone again," Angela said while unsnuggling herself from Bodine. She had turned off her cell phone last night, hoping to get some sleep.

"Hi Mom," Stephen said. "They let me go home last night, and it was too late to call you. I'm at work already."

"Are you feeling all better, Stephen? You didn't get much sleep last night, did you?"

"I slept in the ER from the time they inserted the IV. I was half asleep talking to you last night. I feel pretty good. This is a half day for me anyway. I'll have a big lunch here at the hospital and go on home after that."

"I'm glad you're feeling better," Angela said, "but don't overdo it. We might go to the beach once we get moving this morning. I'll have my phone on if you need me."

"I'm OK, Mom. Love you."

"I love you, too, bye."

Bodine was still under the covers with his "My Wife Works Me So Hard" look on his face. Angela gave him a tickle and pulled the covers off him.

"A few more ZZZ's please?"

Angela covered him back up, and went to shower, dress and start breakfast. By the time Bodine came downstairs, Angela had breakfast ready and she was on the phone with Laura.

"How many messages did he leave?" Angela asked.

"More than ten. I lost count. 'I'm sorry Baby, please call me.' 'I'll never hit you again.' 'Please call me.' 'Are you all right?' It started to sound pathetic. Angela, he's a child. What does he know about real women?" Laura asked.

"Are you going to call him?"

"The only thing I want from him is the clothing I left. I might send him an email after I get back to Vegas. Let him suffer."

"How many more hours until you reach Memphis?" Angela asked.

"I'll be there in three to four hours. Jackson said he's cleaning house."

"Remember, no sex until you tell him. It would be a real deal breaker if he found out about the Herpes afterwards," Angela said.

"OK, Mama, I'll be a good girl."

"All right, I gotta feed this man and kidnap him to the beach. Talk to you soon," Angela said.

* * * *

Angela and Bodine had a great day for the beach, eighty degrees and sunny, with little traffic getting to Wrightsville Beach in the middle of the week. It was a good day for surfing. They watched the surfers, splashed a little in the frigid waves, ate shrimp po-boys on the beach and returned to Raleigh long before dark.

Bodine was feeling mellow enough to pull out the Super Scrabble game. He was good at the "short game;" he could play two or three letters in a corner somewhere, and rack up ninety points. Angela liked to play her "long game," surprising Bodine by using all seven letters when he thought he was winning. Angela liked to use golf terms, about the only thing she learned from six weeks of golf lessons. It usually took them three hours to complete the Super Scrabble game. They took an intermission for dinner, and decided to leave the rest of the game for the next day.

Angela wanted to post some beach pictures on her blog, so she went upstairs expecting to spend fifteen minutes. Her email had a notification of a new comment on her blog. When she saw it was from Paulo, her heart sank. "Angela, have you heard from QTEE?" Angela wouldn't tell him anything, but now she was afraid to post a next blog entry since it would show they were back in North Carolina. She decided she would not allow that man to control her life, too. She ignored his comment and posted her pictures from the beach. She liked the one with a profile of Bodine with the surfers off in the distance. Before she could review it after posting, a new comment popped up, "I know you're there. Please don't ignore me." Then another, "Tell me where is Laura." And another, "She has to talk to me."

By the time Angela stopped shaking and changed her blog settings to require moderation on all comments, Paulo had posted nearly twenty comments. Angela thanked God Paulo was over four thousand miles away, and she was glad Laura had gotten away from him. Now she worried about posting anything on Facebook. Paulo wasn't on her friend's list, but he might be able to see some of her postings as a friend of a friend. She would have to find a way to block him. She hated for her heart to be racing and her brain to be on overload so close to bedtime. It would ruin her sleep.

Bodine stepped in and asked when she was going to bed. It was his way of saying, "Come to bed." So she gave him a wink and shut down the computer. She shut off her cell phone for good measure, and hoped for a quiet day tomorrow. Bodine would get her mind off Paulo.

CHAPTER ELEVEN

Screen Name: TheGuy

Angela had known Lester "TheGuy" online long before she met Bodine. He was her go-to person when she had questions about web page design. Back in the early days of Blackplanet.com, many people tried to hook-up their pages with animations, sparkly words, and music. At first, many of her online friends had midi music, so their visitors heard the sound of a toy piano playing music from their page. Next people started downloading music from Napster before it was shut down for copyright violation. Then some people like TheGuy knew how to play music on their page from CDs in their personal collection. They didn't know it continued to be a copyright violation until ordinary people started being hauled into court for sharing music on the internet. But in those days of innocence, Angela asked TheGuy to hook her up with the code to put Tuck & Patti's "Take My Breath Away" on her Blackplanet page. TheGuy had his own website with tutorials on how to do HTML. In addition, he had his internet biography that started with the story of how he became "TheGuy."

He said when he was in high school, he noticed the popular fellows had all the girls, so he hung out with the popular fellows, thinking he would get some of the girls, too. It didn't work. He realized the popular fellows were on at least one of the sports teams. So Lester decided he would go out for football. Now Lester was never an athletic type, but he practiced with the team and he was there for all the games, mostly keeping the bench warm. His mom would go to all the games hoping to see her son at least touch the ball a few times. And he did. He touched the ball a few times. One Saturday morning, after his mom had sat through a game in the cold stadium the night before, she said to her son, "Lester, I think you just want to play football so you can be one of the guys." He responded, "Mom, I *am* The Guy."

The only time Lester called Angela on the phone was to return a call she had made to him. So when he called Saturday morning, Angela dropped what she was doing to run and answer.

"My goodness, if it isn't TheGuy. How you doing?"

"Hey Angela. I don't usually call married ladies unless their husband is part of the conversation, so would you put Bodine on the line with you?"

"Sure," Angela said. "He considers you a friend to us both, but I'll get him."

When Angela yelled for Bodine, he wondered what it was all about, but he picked up in the bedroom, "Hey TG, How's it going?"

"Everything is fine here," TheGuy said. "I just felt I needed to let Angela know what's being said about her on Facebook."

Angela was stunned. "About me? What?"

"You know that group you set up for BK folks to get together? There's this person named Paulo Ochoa who's been on there the last couple of days saying you know what happened to QTEE and you're not telling."

Angela sighed. "Yes, he's right. I do know, and I decided to let Laura tell her own business."

"So you know where she is?" TG asked.

"Can I trust you to keep this quiet?" Angela asked.

"Everybody wants to know."

"Laura doesn't want Paulo to know where she is."

"Oh, I see. It's like that," TG said.

"And there's the issue of her other relationships," Angela said. "It's too messy to put all her business out there on Facebook."

"Where is she?"

"Let's just say she's on her way back home," Angela said. "And I'm afraid if Paulo knows, he'll start harassing her like he's been doing to me."

"He's been harassing you?"

"Phone calls, Facebook messages, and a flood of comments on my blog," Angela said. "It's starting to rattle me every time the phone rings."

"You want me to send one of my boys to take care of him?"

119

"You got any boys in Rio?" Angela knew the minute the word Rio left her lips she shouldn't have said it.

"Rio? QTEE went to Rio?" TG asked.

Angela feared that tidbit would be too juicy to keep quiet. "Please don't tell it. Keep the Rio part out of it. When Laura says it's OK, you will be the first to know...After Bodine of course."

"Bodine," TG said, "you still there? You're being quiet over there."

"I prefer to stay out of Laura's private life," Bodine replied, "but while I have you on the phone, I gotta tell you, our pastor preached about Noah last Sunday. When he got to the part about gopher wood, Angela poked me, and we both had to stifle our laughter. The dissertation of yours about the Ark is a classic. To this day, you can't find anymore gopher wood because Noah used it all up. Ha Ha Ha."

TG said, "I've had to tone down some of my attacks on Jesus freaks since I joined the church."

"You know Angela and I are active in the church, but we don't believe in those literal interpretations. They can be over the top," Bodine said.

"I don't see you much online lately," TG said.

"You know we've been traveling," Bodine said. "And now I'm trying to get the garden back in shape. Next rainy day, I'll be right there."

"OK man. And Angela, I'll be discreet."

"Thanks, Lester," Angela said.

Screen Name: PattiMelt

Was it everybody's day to check in? This time it was Patti (PattiMelt). Patti and Laura had been good friends online for years. When Patti's son Garnett received a basketball scholarship to UNLV, Patti was overjoyed. She had been a single mother for so long, she was happy to see her son grow up and out of the way. Nevertheless, she cyber-cried on everybody's shoulder about how far Las Vegas was from New Jersey, and she worried about the trouble he could get into in Sin City. Laura volunteered to be his second mom. Since Garnett and Carlton were about the same age, he invited Garnett and his teammates over for dinner every weekend. It became a regular thing. The boys would get a home-cooked meal, and Laura would let them know they had someone nearby they could count on. Laura would report back to Patti about their conversations and assure Patti Garnett wasn't getting into any trouble. Laura never asked for anything in return, but Patti would make sure she had the latest makeup from Mary Kay.

Patti called after Angela finished talking to Lester.

"Hey Ms. Angela."

"Patti, when have I talked to you?" Angela responded.

"It's been awhile."

"Did Lester tell you to call me?"

"He told me he talked to you about Laura, and when I asked if Laura was all right, he said I should talk to you," Patti said.

"Yes, I know how close you and Laura are."

"She hasn't called me in a long time, and she shut off her

phone. I used to count on talking to Laura whenever I felt like it, or she would call me to talk."

"I'm starting to understand what Laura felt when she went away," Angela said. "She had so many people leaning on her, it got to be too much and she needed a break."

"She talked to you, didn't she? You were her favorite." Patti said. Angela could hear the hurt in Patti's voice.

"I don't know about favorites," Angela said. "I got involved after Carlton called me. I don't know why he picked me out of all the members of BK, but he did. There are times when I wish I had been away that day. You would not believe all the phone calls I've been getting."

"And I'm one more," Patti said.

"You can help me figure out a way to let some people know what's going on without telling other people she wants to ignore."

"I get the picture," Patti said. "You want to know who you can trust with certain information."

"Exactly," Angela said. "I was going to wait and let Laura tell it herself in whatever way she wants to tell it. But since she hasn't been online lately, she doesn't get people asking questions all the time. Know what I mean?"

Patti said, "The next time you talk to QTEE, tell her to give you a list of who she trusts, and she needs to come out of hiding long enough to let people know she still cares about them, even if BK is gone."

"OK, I'll do that. But I'll tell her it was you and Lester who made the suggestion," Angela said. "I hope that helps. You know I don't tell people's secrets, but I also know people care enough to want to help."

"Thanks Angela. I hope you let us know something soon," Patti said.

"I'll do my best."

CHAPTER TWELVE

Trouble Out Back

"Bodine, where are you?" Angela looked out the back window, and there he was digging in the dirt. After those last two calls, she was ready to give in. She went outside and followed behind Dusty, watching Bodine from the border of the garden until he looked her way.

"What's up?"

"Not me," Angela said. "I'm ready to run away from home. You want to come with me?"

"Poor honey. What happened now?"

Angela told him about the call from Patti so soon after the call from Lester. "I understand now why Laura had to get away. She had become so wrapped up in everybody else's lives she didn't have room for her own. Now I'm up to my eyeballs in it. I surrender."

"Why don't we take a vacation from Facebook, and let all those people deal with it without us."

"That sounds better all the time."

Angela looked up and saw her brother, Maxwell coming through the gate.

"I rang the bell and when nobody answered, I started to leave," he said, "but then I heard talking back here." He started to sing Beethoven's "Ode to Joy" at the top of his lungs. "I'm so excited about the concert I'm going to do at St. Andrew's. I brought you tickets and you have to come."

Angela said, "Of course we will. When is it?"

"It's next month on a Sunday afternoon."

"I'll put it on the calendar. You came all the way over here to bring the tickets?"

"I was on my way home from rehearsal, and I was all excited about it," Maxwell said.

"Will it be your concert as a soloist or is the choir singing, too?"

"It's actually the choir's concert, but I'll have four solos. I haven't sung this much in years." Angela's brother was a retired music professor. She could see how much this meant to him. Maxwell continued, "What are you two doing out here? I usually see Bodine working the garden, and you inside."

Angela laughed. "It's such a nice day, I needed some fresh air. Besides, Dusty needed some company following Bodine around the garden."

Maxwell said, "He's a good dog to stay out of the vegetables."

"He gets zapped if he crosses the line," Angela said.

"That's mean," Maxwell said.

Bodine said, "He's been zapped once, and it was a low dose. It was enough for him to remember, and he hasn't crossed the line since. We could shut the thing off, and he would never know. I'm trying to figure a way to put collars on the squirrels to keep them out, too."

"That could get to be expensive," Maxwell said.

"Yeah," Bodine said. "Buck shot is cheaper."

Angela heard a loud crack from the woods behind the house, as Bodine fell to the ground.

"My God," she yelled as she knelt to the ground to see what had happened. Bodine held his side in pain, as blood oozed all over his shirt. Maxwell grabbed his cell phone and called 911. Angela removed her shirt and used it to apply pressure to Bodine's side.

Maxwell said into the phone, "My brother has been shot...716 Neuse Arbor...no A-R-B-O-R...no in Raleigh."

Angela tried to keep herself from crying, "Oh no, there are too many Neuse streets. Max, hold this while I push the buttons on the house alarm." She directed Max to continue the pressure on Bodine's wound and ran into the house. When she came back, she had grabbed a fresh shirt from the laundry room and put it on. "I pushed all the buttons, police, fire and rescue. Bodine, what are you feeling?"

"Pain. I've been shot. Is our neighbor Ponzi outside?" Bodine asked.

"Max, go see two doors down with the fire truck. Hold on baby.

Somebody is coming. Talk to me."

"Where's Dusty, is he OK?" Bodine asked.

"He's right here with his head down," Angela said.

Max came running back with Ponzi, who brought his medic kit. "Keep applying pressure. I checked the police radio. Someone is on the way. Hold on there, Bo."

In a few minutes, vehicles with alarms and flashing lights jammed the cul-de-sac. The medics were first knocking on the door. Angela had to head them off to keep them from breaking the door in. Before anyone else could get it together, the EMS team had Bodine on a stretcher, his chest wrapped, and an IV in his arm. They asked which hospital to go to.

Angela said, "Wake Med."

By then the police had come into the backyard to question Angela and Maxwell. What time, what did you see, what did you hear. Angela and Max rattled off so many answers they hardly knew what they were saying. When they had repeated themselves a third time, Angela asked if she could go to the hospital to find her husband.

"Yes ma'am, he should be at Wake Med by now. An officer will come to talk to your husband when he is able to talk."

Angela asked Max to check the house and lockup so she could go; she couldn't remember if she had something cooking or ironing. "And put Dusty in his crate before you go."

"I think I'll stay in the house with Dusty until you come back. He could use the company, and so could I."

"Thanks, Max." Angela drove off to the hospital, praying all the way.

It took over an hour for Angela to find Bodine. She had to undergo security screening, and another round of the same questions because of the shooting. They kept trying to make it into a "drive-by shooting" despite Angela's protestation that they were in the backyard, and the shot came from the woods. And no, Bodine didn't have any enemies. When she could finally see him, he was all cleaned up, wrapped up, and sitting up watching television.

"Sweetie, what did they do to you?"

"They didn't find a bullet," Bodine said. "They X-rayed me to be sure. It must have pierced my side and gone out the back. They stitched me up real good and put me on antibiotics. The police had to come and ask a bunch of stupid questions...what was I doing outside...who would want to shoot me?...Do you own a gun?...does your wife have a gun? I had to laugh at that one. I told them my little Chuckie won't even be in the same room with a gun."

"How are you feeling? Are you in a lot of pain?" Angela asked.

"They have me doped up pretty good. I'll be drifting off any minute now, if the police are finished with me."

"OK, Sweetie you get some rest. I'll see if I can find the doctor."

Angela went to the nurse's station to see what they would tell her. At first they wouldn't say anything until Angela showed them the HIPAA release Bodine had signed years ago so she would be able to get medical information about him. All they could tell her was what Bodine had already told her. They gave her the attending doctor's name and phone number. They had his condition listed as stable. They said in a case like this, they kept a patient at least 24 hours for observation.

Angela found a quiet place to call the doctor, and left a message for him to return the call. She checked on Bodine again, and found him sleeping. All the monitors were beeping away. She decided to go on home and come back early in the morning.

Back home, Max was sitting on the front porch with Dusty sitting at his feet. Dusty perked up when Angela arrived. She told Max what she knew from the hospital and she hoped to get a callback from the doctor. Otherwise, Bodine appeared to be in good hands.

Max said, "We came out here to get away from the phone. I answered one from Laura, one from Patti, and then I gave up answering it. I left notes by the phone in the kitchen from the calls I answered. There may be some messages on your machine."

"Did you tell them Bodine was shot?"

"No, I said you were out. No need to have rumors circulating before we know his condition. I did call Aaron and Stephen to let them know you were at the hospital with Bodine."

"Thanks Max. How did Dusty do?"

"He's a good dog. I didn't know if I should feed him or what to feed him."

"He had his dinner before all the excitement started. He doesn't complain much. I was surprised how quiet he got after the shooting. Poor baby, he could use some petting. Come here Dusty."

Angela didn't often put Dusty in her lap, but this time they both needed some petting.

Max said, "I'll help you lock up, and be on my way. I hope Bodine will be recovered in time for my concert."

"Oh yes, it's been quite a day since you came over here singing."

* * * *

The notes from Max said Laura checked in from Memphis, and Patti asked if she talked to Laura. Angela saw the light flashing on the answering machine and thought she had better listen to the messages. Lester wanted to know what Laura said. There were several hang-ups. Then a loud pop of lightning struck and the lights went off. Angela had her cell phone in her pocket and used the light from it to rifle through the junk drawer in the kitchen until she found a flashlight. After she waited a few minutes for the lights to come back on, she called the emergency number to report an outage.

I might as well go to bed. No computer, no noise from the cordless phones, and no light to read by. I should celebrate the quiet. She called Bodine at the hospital to see how he was doing. When there was no answer in his room, she decided he was sleeping. She checked on Dusty again before going upstairs and found him sleeping, too.

Angela slept soundly for several hours until her cell phone rang. The power company left a recorded update on the outage. Lights should be back by six a.m. *They had to wake me up to tell me.* Getting back to sleep was not easy; she was worried about Bodine. The doctor still hadn't called back. What if the outage went beyond her neighborhood and this whole part of town was in the dark? Then there was another pop, loud enough to shake the house and a downpour so loud it was as if the bottom had fallen out. Bodine would have said it was raining elephants and horses. Then there was a crack Angela couldn't explain. She hoped the roof wasn't going to cave in. Now she was wide awake enough to go around the house with her flashlight and check for any storm damage. She didn't notice any leaks or breaks on the second floor, so she went downstairs and checked. Dusty had his paws over his head and was shaking. She didn't want to let him out of his crate until daylight, because he would want to go out, and she wasn't going out in the storm. She talked baby talk to Dusty to calm him and calm herself at the same time. When the lights came on, it was 5:15 a.m. All the lights she had left on before the power failure were shining bright and the TV in the kitchen was buzzing.

Dusty, at least we can see now. Angela continued checking for damage downstairs until she looked out the front window. A tree in the front yard was split and hanging across the porch. She would have to check for outside damage after she could see. Her cell phone rang again. Another message from the power company checking to see if her power was back. She pressed two on the phone for yes and hung up.

"Dusty, I'll get some clothes on and take you out in a little bit, OK?"

Dusty yipped.

Sunday Morning Crowd

Angela stepped outside through the garage and inspected the damage to the tree. It would survive after a pruning, but there was damage also to the roof of the garage. It was the kind of thing she hadn't had to worry about since marrying Bodine, since he took care of all the handyman repairs. She would have to move some branches to get her car out of the garage. Dusty was her first order of business. He needed his walk. Angela took the short route around the block with him, taking her cell phone along to make some calls. It was too early to call most people, but she thought she would try Bodine's son Nathan and let him know what had happened.

"Good morning, Nathan. I hope I didn't wake you."

"Hey Angela, no I was up already. I was wondering if you would call. I saw the news report of the shooting in your neighborhood."

"You did? What did it say?" Angela asked. "We had a storm last night and the power was out until a little while ago."

"One of my Facebook friends posted it. They said an elderly man was shot in your subdivision, and the police suspected a hunter had fired a gun in the woods near you. Was it somebody you know?"

"It was your dad," Angela said.

"Dad? Is he all right?" Nathan asked.

"He's in the hospital. They said the bullet grazed him. They X-rayed and couldn't find a bullet in him. They bandaged him up and gave him antibiotics and pain meds. He was sleeping when I left last night. They want to keep him 24 hours for observation."

"I never thought of Dad as an elderly man," Nathan said.

"Me neither. But can I get you to call your uncles and your grandmother to let them know he's fine."

"I sure will. Did you have any damage from the storm?"

"We have a tree down and some shingles off the roof of the garage," Angela said.

"You want me to come down and check on it?"

"That would be great," Angela said. "I was thinking of calling a handyman, but your dad would be trying to do it himself. He doesn't need to be climbing ladders until his wound heals."

"I'll take off tomorrow and see if Ernest and Oscar can come, too."

"You're a sweetheart, Nathan."

Dusty had finished his business by then and Angela was turning into the cul-de-sac when she spotted the traffic in front of her house. Neighbors were standing in the front yard, a TV van from WRRD, and a police car were in the driveway. *Oh no. I was hoping to get a quick bowl of oatmeal before going to the hospital.*

The neighbors approached Angela first. Ponzi asked if he could help with the tree, Bennie said he had a tarp to put over the roof of the garage in case it rained again. Angela thanked them as a female police officer approached her. The TV cameras appeared to be rolling.

The officer introduced herself, "I'm officer Cramden. Are you Mrs. Beaudoin?"

Angela said, "Yes, can we go inside?" Angela led her in, and took Dusty to his crate in the kitchen. Angela started a pot of coffee and invited the officer to sit in the kitchen.

"Can you tell me what happened here yesterday?"

"I gave a statement to a couple of officers yesterday here and at the hospital," Angela said.

"I just want to be clear on the details."

"My husband and I..."

"What is your husband's name?" officer Cramden asked.

"Nathan Beaudoin Senior, but our friends call him Bodine or Bo for short. Bodine and my brother Maxwell Platte were in the backyard talking when we heard a loud crack from the woods out back, and my husband fell to the ground bleeding. My brother called 911 from his cell phone and couldn't get them to understand our address, so I ran inside and pushed the buttons on this security panel."

"You pushed fire, police and rescue?" the officer asked.

"That's right. My husband was on the ground bleeding and the 911 operator had trouble understanding Neuse Arbor," Angela said.

"Did you see the gun?"

"I didn't look into the woods at all. After my husband fell, I was attending to him."

"Do you own a gun, Mrs. Beaudoin?"

"No I don't."

"What is your husband's condition?" the officer asked.

"I thought you could tell me. He was sleeping when I left the hospital last night, and you were here before I could call to check this morning. I would like to get dressed so I can go to see him."

The phone rang, and the Caller ID announced, "Call from Memphis, TN."

The officer said, "Would you like to get the phone, ma'am?"

"It's probably a friend calling." Angela said. "I don't need to talk to her right now. I want to check on my husband, if you don't mind. Do you mind if I finish dressing and you can follow me to the hospital if you have more questions."

"I think that's all we need at this time. You have a good day."

When Angela let the officer out, the TV reporter was on the porch with a cameraman. Angela wanted to close the door in their faces, but she started picturing what it might look like on the morning news. She stepped outside to speak to them.

"Mrs. Beaudoin, can we get a statement?" the reporter asked.

"Good Morning, Dave," she said, recognizing the reporter from TV, "could I get you to ride with me to the hospital to see my husband? I need to freshen up my face and I'll be out through the garage in ten minutes." Angela stepped back inside and closed the door before Dave could respond.

Angela took her time collecting herself, finished her coffee and toast, and met the TV people in the garage twenty-five minutes later. Someone had moved the tree branches so she could back out of the garage. She stopped to let Dave into the passenger side of her car.

"Do you mind if my cameraman rides in the backseat?" Dave asked.

"It would be difficult to drive with that kind of distraction," Angela said. "I'm already distracted with worry about my husband. If your cameraman will follow in the van, we can make a quick statement after I get out in front of the hospital."

Angela answered the same questions from Dave she had gotten from the police. She hoped she could still avoid the TV camera. By the time they reached the hospital, Dave was on the phone with the cameraman. One of them had word of a bigger story, a train wreck in downtown Raleigh. When Dave jumped from the car, he thanked Angela for the interview. Angela sent up a very loud, "Thank you Lord."

Bodine was sitting in a chair dressed in his dirty clothes from the day before when Angela reached the room. Angela wished she had had the presence of mind to bring him some fresh clothes. Nevertheless, she was happy he would be going home.

"Good morning, Sweetie. Did the doctor discharge you?"

"I haven't seen a doctor, and if he doesn't get here soon, I'm going to discharge myself," Bodine said.

"I haven't heard from the doctor at all, and I want to talk to him before you leave here. We had a storm last night and the power was out until this morning. I missed a bunch of calls."

"Is QTEE still calling?"

"I think she tried this morning while I was talking to the police, but I didn't answer. I'll call her after you get home and settled."

"What did the police want this morning?" Bodine asked.

"The same questions they asked last night. Wasting my time. Let me go down the hall and see if I can find the doctor. Don't go anywhere."

Angela went to the nurse's station and asked about the doctor. They told her he makes his rounds after lunch. She asked if the nurse assigned to Bodine would please come to his room, explain his condition, and prepare his discharge papers. When she asked for the name and number of the patient advocate, the nurses started looking for the doctor's phone number. "You may be able to reach Dr. Weeks at this number," the nurse on duty said as she handed Angela a card with the doctor's number. Angela called the number while standing at the nurse's station, and left a message for the doctor saying the patient advocate insists that Mr. Beaudoin get his discharge papers before he leaves this morning.

Angela went back to Bodine's room and sat with him watching Sunday morning television shows, while they waited. The doctor arrived at 10:15 a.m.

Mr. Beaudoin, Mrs. Beaudoin, I was not able to reach you last night. I understand you had a power outage."

"You had my cell phone number, Doctor, and it was on all night."

"Oh...well this is what we have. Mr. Bodine has a deep wound in his side. He lost a lot of blood, and he still needs bed rest."

"Does he have any internal injuries?" Angela asked.

"No, he was very lucky. Of course, his extra padding protected him from any injury to organs, but he has deep tissue involvement. I want him to continue the pain medication for three days. Even if he says he feels fine, I want him to stay in bed for three days. Today is day one. You stay in bed Sunday, Monday and Tuesday. On Wednesday you can get up and around, walk outside if you feel like it. No heavy lifting."

Angela interrupted, "No climbing ladders, and no workout at the gym."

"Right," the doctor said. "The wound needs to close completely before you do any climbing or workouts."

Bodine said, "OK, fine. Just get me out of here."

"The nurse will be in shortly to change your bandage, and show your wife how to care for your injury. She'll have your discharge instructions," the doctor said before he left.

CHAPTER THIRTEEN

The Patient

Angela knew Bodine would not be patient. As she pulled the car into the cul-de-sac, he saw the mess of branches and leaves in the yard, and the bright blue tarp on the roof of the garage.

"You know I have to take care of that," he said.

Angela said, "Help is on the way. Nathan said he would be here tomorrow. I know you taught him everything you know, so he'll fix it up in no time."

All Bodine could say was, "Humph."

Angela concluded he must be exhausted since he didn't object to getting in the bed while she made him a cup of tea and gave him the TV remote. She checked his bandage before she tucked him in. She was hardly out of the room before he was asleep, but Angela left the TV on in case he woke up.

Now that Angela was home again, she decided to take a few minutes to write a Facebook note to give an update on Bodine, and ask their friends not to call for a couple of days so he can get the rest he needs. She saw Nathan had posted something on Facebook already, and Bodine's wall was full of good wishes for his quick recovery. She knew Dusty needed a walk, but she didn't want to leave Bodine alone in the house. She hated leaving Dusty in the backyard to do his business, so she walked him slowly down to the corner and talked him into getting done.

"You're such a smart dog, Dusty-boo, you'll get a special treat," Angela said as she scooped his mess into a plastic bag. "Papa will be proud of you."

Poor Dusty was all off his schedule, and had not eaten anything all day, so Angela poured his special blend into his dish, and let him hang out on the deck in the back while she started dinner. Once the meal was cooking and Dusty was in his crate, she set about to make a few calls. First was Bodine's mother to let her know he was home and resting. She had left a message for Nathan on Facebook about the tree and garage. She dreaded calling QTEE. Angela needed some time to herself, but she needed to get this over with.

"Hey Laura, I don't know if you've heard what happened to Bodine."

"Patti called me and told me about a shooting. Is he all right?" Laura asked.

"I just brought him home from the hospital. He's supposed to stay in bed until Wednesday. Did Patti also tell you about the conversations I had with her and Lester?"

"You mean about telling people where I am?" Laura asked.

"Yes."

"Do I have to?"

"Yes you do," Angela said. "I'm tired of keeping your secrets and Paulo is telling people I'm not telling what I know. You should be able to tell the people you trust without letting Paulo know where you are."

"I've been having such a nice quiet visit with Jackson," Laura said. "I didn't want to have to mention Paulo. I told him about Brazil. I didn't name Paulo by name. When he told me about Bonita, I laughed so much I thought I would wet my pants. And we talked about health issues. I haven't worked up to the big one yet."

"You know, I've been getting so many calls I'm starting to understand why you ran away," Angela said. "When you talked to Patti did she tell you about her conversation with me? I think she felt left out of your life when she didn't know what was going on."

"I understand what you're saying. I need to make some calls. I don't want to get online and start the whole BK thing up again. Jackson is more mellow than he's ever been. I don't want to disturb this thing we have going right now."

"And no sex?" Angela asked.

"Honest to God," Laura said. "I'm having trouble believing it myself. Part of it is he's not really in good health. I asked him to let me go with him to his next doctor appointment, which is on Wednesday. He said he would. Meanwhile I got my doc in New York to call in a script for me for those generic antivirals you were talking about.

"I asked him why he didn't prescribe those in the first place. He said he didn't see many patients with Herpes, or at least he didn't know about many. He did check the PDR while he had me on the phone and said it would solve my problem. I'll start taking them today. By Wednesday, I'll be able to discuss some things with Jackson's doctor."

"Let me go so you can make those calls, and I can make sure I'm not burning dinner," Angela said.

Angela looked up, and there was Bodine, checking on her pots and looking in the oven.

"You're supposed to be resting," she said.

"I started smelling real food, and I got hungry," Bodine said.

Angela showed him to the table and gave him a glass of water and his next dose of medication. "Dinner will be ready shortly."

"I see you haven't freed yourself yet."

"I'm working on it." And she gave him a kiss. "See how quiet it's been around here this afternoon."

The phone rang. Angela groaned, "I jinxed it." She eyed the Caller ID and said, "I forgot to tell the pastor. Do you want to talk to him?" She handed the phone to Bodine, who chatted with the pastor and told him about their excitement from yesterday. Angela finished getting dinner ready and set the table.

She heard Bodine say, "And I didn't even get on TV."

They had another quiet spell before the phone rang again. Thinking it was Laura; she picked it up quickly and said, "What is it this time?"

"It's me," Jackson said. "Laura had to go pick up a prescription. I wanted to thank you, while she's gone. You were so right about taking it slow. This is the best few days I have ever spent with her, and we're connecting on a level we never have before. All anybody wants in this world is to know they were loved.

"I had my career, and I was good at what I did, but even having the material success doesn't come anywhere near knowing that woman really loves me. You know I was starting to think of you as our own personal matchmaker. Laura and I joked about it. But you know if I don't see tomorrow, I thank God for this priceless gift, knowing Laura and I have found a love."

Angela felt her eyes grow wet as a warmth settled into her heart, "Man you're making me cry."

* * * *

Nathan arrived Monday morning, along with Bo's brothers, Ernest and Oscar. Angela had to shush them and remind them Bodine needed his rest. She didn't want him getting out of bed trying to supervise the repairs. She had to make Bodine promise not to come downstairs. It was difficult keeping him away from Dusty, and Dusty looked lonesome for Bodine. Whenever he heard Bodine's voice, he would whine. Angela decided to take up her post on the front porch so she could watch the action and Dusty could sit in her lap. He panted happily and wagged his tail. Angela couldn't wait to tell Bodine Dusty loved her best.

The fixit team cut the tree branches into manageable pieces and put them in garbage bags to be picked up next week. Angela provided sandwiches for their break before they tried to tackle the roof. She knew if she fed them she would have to feed Bodine, otherwise she would see his nose pressed against the upstairs window. Dusty had his share of the snacks too. Angela hoped he wouldn't get diarrhea from being off his usual diet. She didn't need another patient. She gave him a few dog biscuits hoping real solid food would counteract the effects of all the Cheetos. They took one of the pieces of roofing the storm had blown to the ground to Lowes to get a matching pack of replacement shingles. Once they got back to work, they were finished in no time.

Nathan and his helpers were all grungy when they finished, so Angela set them up in the bathrooms with body wash and towels. Bodine came downstairs at about the time his brothers were finished cleaning up. He needed to check behind their work before they left. Angela had to allow him that. She knew he wouldn't be happy if he didn't. Nathan took over from there and took the brothers out for food, promising to bring something back for Bodine and Angela.

Angela got Bodine back upstairs and helped him shower, keeping his bandage dry with a wrapping of Saran Wrap. She changed his dressing and saw the wound looked better than the day before, but was still wet and oozy. She hoped it would be dried up by Wednesday when Bodine would insist upon getting back outside. Today he was mostly bored, wanting to get back to his gardening.

"How about finishing our old game of Scrabble?" Angela said. "I'll let you sit up in your recliner for a while."

"I'd rather have my laptop up here."

Angela said, "Ok, but only for an hour. You shouldn't be moving about as much as you have been." She got the laptop and set up the side desk for him. A little Facebook couldn't hurt. When the gang came back, Angela and Bodine went to the kitchen to eat the Chinese takeout they brought. Bodine had hoped for fried chicken, but he ate all they gave him. It was good talking and kidding with his brothers for a while. But Angela could see he was getting tired, and insisted he get back to bed. Bodine didn't argue. He went back to bed and fell fast asleep.

Nathan looked worried. "Is Dad going to be all right? He looks tired."

"He's still on antibiotics and pain medicine," Angela said. "I don't know if he's still having much pain, but the doctor wanted to make sure he got the rest he needs for the wound to heal. If his wound isn't looking healed by Wednesday, I'm going to take him back to the doctor. I'll stay on top of it."

"I know you will," Nathan said. "We'll get out of your way and get on back to Maryland. I'll tell Grandma how he's doing."

Angela gave Nathan and the brothers a group hug and sent them on their way.

Tuesday Morning

Angela woke to the sound of Dusty whining to get out. Since Bodine was still fast asleep, she slipped into the jeans she wore last night, and pulled a jacket over her nightie and went downstairs to take Dusty out. When Angela stepped out into the humid spring morning, she felt her hair and remembered she hadn't combed it. At least she had her cell phone in her pocket. She tried using the shiny side of the phone to see what her hair looked like. It's a good thing she kept it short. She could rake her fingers through it and make it somewhat presentable. The neighborhood kids were gathering at the corner waiting for the school bus. They never paid her any attention anyway, but Dusty went sniffing around between them, so they had to look up. She hoped Bodine would stay asleep until she came back. She needed to walk an hour to make up for all the exercise she had missed the last few days. Dusty wouldn't mind at all. He would be ready for a nap when they got back.

A few neighbors were out walking. Jim passed her talking on his cell phone and waved as he went by. The group of ladies from a few streets over had their regular walking time together. She hadn't seen them since the last homeowners meeting. She said hello and yawned as she went by, but they stopped her and asked about Bodine. They had heard about the shooting.

"Did the police find out who was shooting out there?"

Angela responded, "They haven't told me a thing. If they questioned other people half as much as they questioned me, they would have found something by now. Come to think of it, they never checked our yard or the back of the house for a bullet."

"Didn't Bodine take a bullet?"

"No they X-rayed him at the hospital and didn't find anything," Angela said. "Now that you mention it, I'll check out the backyard to see what I can find. See you ladies later. I need to get back before Bodine wakes up looking for his breakfast."

When Angela and Dusty got back, Bodine was still sleeping. Angela took the opportunity to shower and put on some fresh clothes. She cooked breakfast and went out to explore the backyard. She checked around the spot where Bodine went down and continued walking toward the house, not finding anything. She remembered the big storm they had on the night of the shooting. *The elephants and horses might have buried all the evidence.* She noticed a hole in the door to the tool shed. After she retrieved the key from in the house to unlock the door, she found the hole went all the way through, but she couldn't find a hole in the back wall of the shed.

Angela wracked her brain trying to remember the names of any of the police officers who questioned her. Not one of them had given her a card. The only person she could remember was Dave from the TV station, and she couldn't remember his last name. Bodine was downstairs in the kitchen and coming outside to find her already.

Angela said, "Good morning. How's my Sweetie?"

Most mornings Bodine would give his little boy reply, "I fine," but this time he said, "Bored."

"I have something for you to think about. What happened to the bullet that grazed you? I found a hole in the door to the shed, and I can't find the bullet in the shed. I was going to call the police, but I don't have a name. Then I thought about Dave from TV."

"You mean Dave Harrison?" Bodine said. "How did he get involved?"

"I forgot, I didn't tell you. He showed up Sunday morning when I was on my way to the hospital. I kinda dodged a TV interview by taking him with me, and then he got a bigger story to chase. I should be able to convince him to get the police on the job looking for the bullet. I bet I can find his email address on the internet."

"He's probably on Facebook and Twitter," Bodine said.

"Hey, you're right. Let's sit down and eat, then I'll find old Dave."

After breakfast, Angela put Bodine back to bed and got on her computer. It didn't take much hunting to find Dave's email address, his Facebook page and his Twitter. Angela left messages through all those forms of media. She hoped Dave would jump at the chance for a scoop, but she groaned at the thought of another interview. She started thinking Bodine might like to be interviewed on TV. As long as he didn't overdo it, it might get him out of the doldrums.

Angela stayed on the computer for a while hoping Dave might respond. She caught up with some of the chatter about QTEE. She couldn't find any recent posts from Paulo, and hoped he had given up. After she updated her status, she had some messages from people asking about Bodine, so she posted a Facebook note telling how he was faring. There were many good wishes for him. She let people know he was on bed rest and she didn't want to disturb him. After she shut down her Facebook session, and went about cleaning up the breakfast dishes there was a phone call from a name she didn't understand. When she checked the Caller ID, she could see the voice couldn't pronounce WRDD, and grabbed the receiver.

"Hello Mrs. Beaudoin, this is Dave Harrison from Good Morning Raleigh, I got your message about the bullet. I have a few names at RPD, and I'll find out who is on the case and get back to you. Do you think this time we can get an interview?"

"I think my husband would be happy if they can find the bullet," Angela said. "It may give them a lead to who shot him."

"Is he fearful about being out in the yard?" Dave asked.

"Oh no, he's been on bed rest ever since he was discharged from the hospital. He would love to be out in the yard working in his garden."

"I'll get back to you when I know something," Dave said.

Dusty was sleeping, Bodine was sleeping, and Angela started to think about a nap herself when the phone rang. Another call from Memphis. It was Jackson. He barely said hello before he started in on Angela.

"I know how you said you don't divulge peoples' secrets. But why do I feel like I was set up?"

"What are you talking about?" Angela asked.

"Laura dropped the H-Bomb on me this morning."

"And?"

"You knew all the time," Jackson said.

"I don't know about all the time, but we did talk about it."

"So your plan was to get me all buttered up and feeling all full of love and drop the bomb on me," Jackson said.

"I know it looks like that, but suppose she had told you on the phone before she got to Memphis. What would you have done?"

"Probably would have told her to forget it. She dumped me, I was fine without her."

"And think what you would have missed," Angela said.

"So the matchmaker wins again."

"It's not that way. I think you two could be good for each other. Where is Laura now? Does she know you're mad at me?"

"I'm not mad. I just feel like I've been had," Jackson said.

"Just yesterday you were thanking me."

"Damn, woman. What am I supposed to do now? I have enough ailments already and I don't need another one."

"It's not like it could kill you," Angela said. "Did she tell you about the medication she's taking?"

"She started taking it yesterday. Suppose it doesn't work?"

"You could use a condom. That won't kill you either."

"Goodbye Angela." He hung up before Angela could say anything else.

Tired, Angela went to lie down for a little nap before anybody else called.

Memphis, Jackson's apartment

Laura walked into the room and said, "Hey Babe, I heard you talking on the phone. I thought we were good."

Jackson thought for a while and said, "I don't know, Laura. I wasn't ready for this Herpes thing."

"Neither was I. I thought I was safe, and it happened. I wanted to be up front with you before I exposed you to anything."

"It only reminds me you went all the way to Brazil to be with somebody else," Jackson said.

"I admit I was a fool. It was one of the dumbest things I ever did. I thought we went through this already. I was getting overwhelmed by people on BK needing me all the time. I had to get away, and Brazil was calling. I thought you understood. Do I have to beg?"

"No, no begging required. I guess I need more time to process this whole thing."

Will you still come with me to Vegas?" Laura asked.

"First I need to get through my doctor's appointment tomorrow. I still want you to come with me. You need to hear firsthand what the doctor has to say."

Now Laura frowned. "Are you expecting bad news?"

"I had a bunch of tests, and this is the follow up visit. The doctor hasn't said anything yet. And I guess I'm a little afraid of what he might say. I want you with me. Ask all the questions you want."

"Jackson, you're scaring me."

Jackson pulled Laura to him and held her tight. "Even with all we've been through, you're still the best thing that's ever happened to me."

Laura kissed him and said, "I can't sing like Gladys Knight and the Pips, but you know I love you."

They spent the rest of the day staying close in their non-erotic intimacy. Laura cooked for him, he fed her. Laura started to feel the worst was over. To lighten the mood, she asked Jackson about the Escalade.

"I'm going to turn that hog in for something sporty before we drive to Vegas. What do you think?" Laura asked.

"You should put in a reservation for a Corvette, if that's what you want. We're not in a hurry, are we?"

"I know I'll have a pile of bills to pay when I get back, but another couple of days won't make much difference."

CHAPTER FOURTEEN

Neuse Arbor Way, Raleigh

It was late in the day before the police showed up again with the TV van following close behind. When the doorbell rang, Angela looked out and saw flashing blue lights and a cameraman.

When she opened the door, Angela said to the police, "If you're not making an arrest, could you cut the blue light please? It's disturbing the neighbors."

The police officer agreed to turn off the lights just as Dave Harrison stepped up on the porch. "I thought it would make a nice intro to our interview," he said.

Angela rolled her eyes at Dave and offered him a seat on the porch. The police officer returned as Dave attempted to begin his interview. The police officer introduced himself as Officer Bernard Abrams. "Mrs. Beaudoin, I'm sorry to have to disturb you again, but I understand from Mr. Harrison here you may have located the bullet from the shooting last week."

"That's right. Can I show you?"

Angela took the men to the backyard, and showed them the bullet hole in the door to the shed. The cameraman followed along filming the conversation. Angela opened the shed and said, "I haven't found the bullet. I've been too busy tending to my husband to dig under all this rubble in the shed."

Officer Abrams said, "I have an evidence team scheduled to come before the end of today to go through the shed and find the bullet, if you don't mind. I don't have a search warrant."

"I think my husband would want to watch to make sure nobody breaks any of his toys...uh tools in the process. It's getting dark now, and I would prefer if you could do it in the morning."

"I'll see what we can do."

By this time, Dave was getting peeved at losing his interview. "I went through a lot of trouble to set this up."

Angela said, "It would have helped if you had told me when you were coming instead of just showing up."

"OK, fine."

Angela wasn't usually so short-tempered, but with the shooting, the storm, Jackson and his H-Bomb, she knew she should count to ten before going inside.

At least Paulo has given up, she thought. If only she knew how wrong she was.

Wednesday Morning

Bodine woke up early, whispering to Angela, "Are you awake yet?"

"I am now." Angela had to laugh. He was getting even for all the Christmas mornings she had waken him before dawn. "You're ready to be off bed rest. Let me go pee first. Then I'll check your wound."

Bodine was happy; the wound had closed over, was dry to touch, and he could get out of bed.

"But I have to warn you, you can't start climbing ladders and straining yourself. I'll agree to some non-strenuous activity outside. I'm going to have to watch you like a hawk."

Bodine grinned.

Angela said, "I told you the police are coming back to see if they can find the bullet. You'll have to supervise them. And old Dave will be back trying to get an interview."

"OK."

Angela knew nothing could kill his good mood. It relieved her worry, too. When Dave showed up with a cameraman and a forensics investigator, she said to Bodine, "Have at it, they're all yours." Bodine and Dusty took them into the backyard and they were there until they uncovered the bullet from the debris on the floor of the tool shed. After Dave managed to get only a few sentences out of Bodine, he and his cameraman gave up and left. Dave said he would call the police later for a report.

Angela slipped away for a step class while Bodine was busy in the shed. She knew the exercise was good for her heart, and she could tell the difference as well in her mind. Her memory and attention span improved after a cardio workout. In addition, she slept much better at night.

They didn't expect to hear anything about the bullet, so they were surprised when Dave showed up again. Dave said the bullet was from a hunting rifle.

This time Bodine was ready to talk and was glad Dave could get a cameraman to come on short notice.

"I thought about it after you left and I remembered we had quite a history with shooting in those woods since we built the house in 2002," Bodine said. "Between those sixty-foot Loblolly pines, there is a lot of shorter growth...wild dogwoods and smaller pine trees. It gets rather thick in there like it is now in the spring, but in the fall you can see through the trees.

"The first time I remember hearing shots, it was in the fall when I was building the gazebo out back, someone shot a paintball and it hit my fence near where I was standing. I went back in the woods and found a man with his son practicing with a paintball gun. The man said it was only paint, and I told him he ought to teach his son not to shoot where people might be. I didn't hear any more from them.

"A year or so later there seemed to be shooting back there quite frequently. I called the Raleigh Police Department, and they sent someone out to check. When the officer came, he noted the city had annexed our subdivision, but the surrounding unincorporated area, including the woods, fell under the jurisdiction of the Wake County Sherriff. I called the Sherriff's Department and they came out, but couldn't find anything I should be worried about.

"Now I am worried," Bodine said. "I got shot. Can you help get some action out here?"

Dave said he would follow up with the RPD and the Sherriff, and would report on the air what his findings were.

Angela knew Bodine wasn't worried since they had seen developers staking out that land. The neighborhood rumor-mill said the bulldozers would be coming to clear that area before the end of the year. They would lose the privacy of the woods, but there would be no more hunting ground back there.

At least it kept Bodine busy and not climbing ladders for a couple of days. She snickered when she thought how their friends on Facebook would say a squirrel shot Bodine for revenge.

Memphis, the Office of Dr. Francois Abud

When the receptionist called Jackson in for his appointment, he took Laura with him.

"Doc, this is the special lady in my life, Laura Murchison. I asked her to come with me to my appointment today. Now give me the good news," Jackson said. "I have my lady here holding my hand."

"Can I speak freely in front of Ms. Murchison?" the doctor asked.

"Yes, you can tell her anything you tell me."

"The good news is your stomach cancer is still in remission," the doctor began. "Your blood count is healthy. Your cholesterol is still a little high. I'm going to increase the dosage on your cholesterol medication. Your blood pressure is still too high. I'm adding another medication for blood pressure. Your weight is fine, but all the other signs tell me your diet is not what it should be. You need to eat more vegetables, more fiber. It will improve your cholesterol, your blood pressure, and may help keep your stomach healthy. What do you think, Ms. Murchison?"

Laura said, "I'm glad I came with him. We can both improve on our diet, and I'll do what I can to help him."

"Do you two eat out a lot?" the doctor asked.

"We haven't been together for very long," Laura replied. "I know Jackson doesn't do much cooking, and we've been eating out at least once every day for the last week."

"I won't tell you to stop eating out, but Jackson, you have to eat more vegetables, cut out the fried food, and the red meat. If you can find a cafeteria or a local diner, you can do better than eating at one of those chain restaurants."

Jackson said, "We hear you, Doc. Is that the worst of it?"

"That's the worst of it for now, but if you don't make some big changes in your diet, you will see a lot worse."

Laura asked, "Are you trying to scare him?"

"If that's what it takes."

After they left the doctor, Jackson took Laura to Piccadilly Cafeteria where they could have lots of vegetables. They each had a vegetable plate for lunch. Laura didn't say much, but she smiled her loving smile at Jackson.

"Do you think we can handle this better or worse deal?" Jackson asked.

Laura's eyes widened when she asked, "Are you proposing something?"

Jackson chuckled and finished his lunch.

Back in Raleigh

Angela noticed the phone had rung only once since Dave left and it was a call from her friend Irma asking when the girls could get together for lunch. She told Irma about the shooting, and how Bodine was recovering nicely. She said they might be able to have lunch next week. Angela started to think she was getting her life back. She wondered about Laura and Jackson, but she knew Laura could handle it. By the end of the day, Bodine was tired from being up and around all day, so he agreed to turn in right after dinner. He still had a big grin on his face, and his wound still looked fine.

After Bodine was asleep, Angela took calls from Nathan, Aaron, and Stephen. They were all checking on Bodine since they knew he would be off bed rest. She told them he had had a good day, and had turned in early. Angela didn't feel so pressed to tell the world on Facebook, but she had not been online all day. She planned to post a few greetings to the people she liked to say hello to every day. She hadn't played any of her games since Laura disappeared. She had a few unfinished games of Scrabble if her friends hadn't forced her to default. She said to herself, "This is a good time to go cold turkey. No more Facebook games."

Memphis, Jackson's Apartment

Laura and Jackson had shopped for groceries, and cooked a vegetarian dinner together. Jackson asked, "You're not going to make a vegetarian out of me are you?"

Laura said, "You know how much I love my steak. But we're going to eat extra vegetables whenever we eat meat."

"I can deal with that."

When they had cleaned up the kitchen, Jackson put on some mellow music, a little Barry White, and turned down the lights. He pulled her onto the sofa with him and kissed her. He said, "Abstinence makes the heart grow fonder."

"We don't have to keep abstaining do we?"

"No my dear, I have something else in mind." He slipped out of the room, and started running a bath for her.

"I smell bubbles." Laura said as she entered the bathroom.

"I'm not ready yet," he said.

"I sure am," she said.

* * * *

When Laura and Jackson awoke, they were tangled in each other's arms, tangled in the sheets.

"Aren't we silly," Laura said.

"How do you mean?"

"All the time we've wasted when I could have been loving you like this years ago."

"We'll just have to make up for lost time," Jackson said.

"When are we going back to Las Vegas?"

"Why don't we check on your order for a Corvette, and see if we can be on our way tomorrow?"

"Do you think we can do it in three days? I don't want to push too hard. We can be home Saturday night. What do you think?" Laura asked.

"Sounds like a plan. Call Carlton and tell him to get us some groceries."

"My baby has probably grown a foot since I left. He won't recognize his grandma." Laura started to cry. "Silly me. I lost touch with what's important."

Jackson rolled over on top of her and said, "Let me show you again."

Back to Routine

The doctor had said no heavy lifting for Bodine, but he couldn't stand it anymore. He had to go to the gym. Angela made him promise to stay away from the weights. He could do the treadmill and the elliptical machine while Angela had her class. Bodine said he would go along with it for now, but he made an appointment with his regular doctor for follow-up.

Angela had a new care partner, a woman this time who contracted HIV from a man she had known all her life. Eleanor found out she was HIV positive after she was hospitalized for an assortment of symptoms that made her feel like her body was shutting down. She had been sick so long she had lost her job and had to move in with her sister. When she got the diagnosis, she didn't want to live. Her sister was already her best support, but the Care Team helped her navigate through the services available for HIV patients, including help with paying for the medications. Angela and two other ladies took Eleanor out for dinner a few times and talked about her plans for the future. Eleanor had been focusing on getting her legs working better through physical therapy. She was already obese, and her medications were causing her to retain fluid in her joints. Still Eleanor was encouraged by the Care Team and the women of her church she had confided in. She had started talking about taking charge of her life and moving to New York to enroll in culinary school.

Angela was glad to have her own life back. She hadn't heard from Laura or Jackson in over two weeks, and she didn't call them. The BK group on Facebook settled down to hardly mentioning Laura and there were no posts from Paulo. Angela never said she had ESP but there were times like now when she knew something was about to happen.

The call came. "Call from Las Vegas, NV" This time it was both of them.

"Hi Angela. Where is Bodine? Can you put him on too?" Laura said.

"OK, hold on, I'll get him...Bodine, telephone."

Bodine picked up and joined the conversation.

"We decided to tell you both at the same time," Laura said. "You're the first to know...after Carlton of course. We're getting married and we want you two to be in the wedding."

Bodine let out a "WHOOP," and Angela started to cry. "I'm so happy for you. When are you going to do the thing?"

"We want to get married here in Las Vegas," Laura replied, "and not at one of those chapels Angela dreamed about. As soon as we can get a date at one of the nicer chapels in a hotel on the Strip, we'll check with you on the date."

Bodine said, "You know I love to go to Vegas, but we might have to squeeze you in between some other trips we have planned."

"Why don't you email me the dates you aren't free, so we can do this," Laura said. "I want Angela to be my matron of honor."

Jackson chimed in, "And Bodine, will you be my best man?"

"Of course," Bodine replied.

Angela said, "Just like in my dream."

"Bodine," Jackson said, "it sounds like you and I are the last to know."

Angela made sure she had Laura's current-actual-really-check-everyday-email address. "I'm so excited. Have you decided where you will live?"

Jackson said, "She already signed the condo over to Carlton, so our plan is to live in Memphis."

"So you'll be only halfway across the country. How does Carlton feel about this?" Angela asked.

Laura said, "He's so tired of my antics, he's glad to see me settle down. I've started calling him Daddy. And of course, he'll be the one to give me away."

"This is going to be so special. Are you going to tell the folks online?"

Laura said, "Let's wait until we have a date and a place, and we'll see if we can afford to invite anybody else."

The Rumors

Angela didn't tell a soul about Laura's wedding plans. She had even sworn Bodine to secrecy. The buzzing started in the BK group on Facebook. The headline was "Who was invited to Laura and Jackson's wedding?" TheGuy himself posted this. He had to have heard it from Laura. Angela didn't ask him, but she watched the responses. "When did this happen?" "When is the wedding?" "Where will it be?" "If you're not invited will you crash the party?"

As far as Angela knew, Laura and Jackson had not signed up on Facebook. It was killing her to stay out of it. She had to call.

"Laura, the word is out about the wedding. I swear I didn't say a word to anybody."

"You won't believe this, but it was Bonita," Laura said. "You know Bonita with the gumbo? She spotted us coming out of the wedding chapel at Bellagio. I walked right into her. There was no avoiding her. I tried playing it off by pretending we were just walking around the hotel, but the planner was with us."

"Did she say anything?"

"She looked at Jackson and smacked her lips and said, uh huh."

Angela had to laugh. "No she didn't."

"What are you hearing?" Laura asked.

"Who's invited? Who's going to crash? Somehow, Lester is in the middle of it. Does Lester know Bonita?" Angela asked.

"You know Lester knows every hood rat from BK. He allows himself to be seen with the pretty girls, but he gets all the scoop from the hood rats."

"Were you planning to invite him?" Angela asked.

"We haven't figured out the cost yet, and now we have to look somewhere else. Did you have this much trouble when you and Bodine got married?"

"No way," Angela said. "We had a church wedding and a small reception at the pool house in the subdivision where I lived at the time. I wouldn't know how to have a Las Vegas wedding."

Laura said, "We should go traditional, too. I wonder if we could have it in a church...not one of those 24-hour chapels."

"When was the last time you went to church?"

"Don't get all righteous on me now."

"I'm not being righteous," Angela said. "I just wanted an idea of possibilities."

"I was raised Catholic, but I used to go to a Baptist church about every month."

"How long has it been? Would they recognize you?" Angela asked.

"We're going to have to check it out. I'll let you know."

Angela said, "Before you go, I've been meaning to ask you about Paulo. Did you ever call him back?"

"I thought about it a long time," Laura said. "I was going to get him to send me my stuff, or at least my wallet. Then I remembered I had replaced the urgent items and cancelled the credit cards. I got all my insurance cards replaced, too. The clothes and personal effects, I decided, those are merely things. Besides, I didn't want to talk to Paulo again. Calling him would put him back in my life. I don't need more complications now. I had the land line cancelled since I have my cell phone and I'll be moving to Memphis after the wedding."

"You sure know how to put someone out of your life. You had lots of practice with Jackson," Angela said.

"Girl, don't you go there. I always loved Jackson; I didn't know how to handle it. I think we've got it straight now. I'll talk to you soon."

Angela wanted to tell Lester to back off with his rumors, but it would just feed the fire. She hoped Laura could find a simple solution for her wedding.

Angela had hardly hung up the phone when it rang again.

"Speak of the devil," she whispered before answering the phone. "Hello Lester. What are you up to today?"

"Hey Angela. I didn't mean any harm. I'm happy for Laura."

Angela sensed he was fishing for information. "Have you talked to Laura?"

"Yeah," he said, "she told me she and JackDaniels had set the date."

Now Angela knew he was fishing. Laura didn't have a venue yet.

"Is that so? What's the date?"

"July the fifteenth, at the Bellagio in Las Vegas," Lester said.

"Lester, you should know better than try to get information from me. Now quit it."

"If you would tell me what's going on, I wouldn't have to make up shit," Lester said.

Angela laughed out loud. "You know I love you, Lester. But I can't tell you what I don't know."

"You sure?"

"If you want to get invited to the wedding, you'd best stop spreading rumors, and stay away from those hood rats."

"Now you've gone and started name-calling," Lester said. "Bonita is a nice girl; she's just a bit short of a full deck."

"You wouldn't think of taking her to the wedding, would you?"

"I thought she would make the ideal date for the wedding since she already lives in Vegas. I wouldn't have to pay her way or anything."

"Are you trying to get yourself un-invited before they have even set the date?" Angela asked.

"Maybe I need to start keeping my mouth shut," Lester said.

"Why don't you tell the folks on Facebook all about gopher wood," Angela said.

Lester said, "Say good night, Angela."

Angela said, "Good night, Angela."

CHAPTER FIFTEEN

Las Vegas

Laura had finally solidified the wedding arrangements. Angela and Bodine flew to Las Vegas three days before the big day so Bo could enjoy a few days cruising through all the casinos on the Strip to see what was new. He knew he would see something new under construction, a new wing, a new hotel. Bodine liked to gamble, but he didn't win the way he used to before the Strip became so expensive. They stayed at the Caesars Palace thanks to a deal Bodine received in the mail for player's club members. Angela loved Vegas in the summertime. Her friends thought it was crazy considering the heat in August. She loved hanging out at the pool, and Caesars had her favorite pools. She and Bodine would be up early anyway due to the time zone difference. Their routine was to go to the pool right after breakfast and stake out a spot in the shade, with misters spraying them every ten minutes. Angela enjoyed reading and napping in the shade, and she could dunk in the cool, refrigerated waters to chill her body when the temperature rose into the nineties. Caesars' tall towers provided abundant shade in the morning, and by the time the sun rose high in the sky, it was noon and time to go inside anyway.

This day when Bodine splashed around in the pool, a young woman took the lounge chair next to Angela. Angela said hello, and the young woman, Angela guessed to be barely over twenty-one, smiled and said hello. Angela continued her reading and noticed all the other people around the pool had something to read, had kids to attend to, or napped. All but this young woman. The way she looked made Angela shake her head. Either she didn't know she looked like a hooker, or she didn't care. A young attractive woman with a weave down to her butt, French manicured fingers and toes, and nothing to do but recline on the lounger. After a while, she got up and entered one of the ground floor cabana suites beside the pool area, and came back with an iPod. She played with the iPod for a bit until she found her playlist, lay back, and closed her eyes. Then a man came out of the same cabana suite and reclined on a lounger across the pool from where Angela sat. The young girl still had her eyes closed until he came across, tapped her foot, and motioned for her to join him on his side of the pool. She gathered her towels and followed him. He was a white or light brown man, looked to be in his thirties, bald head, muscular body, a handsome face, and a huge sunburst tattoo that covered his left shoulder from his pectorals in the front, to his shoulder blade in the back. Angela could see by his angry face and flailing hands from her side of the pool that he argued with the girl until he told her to go inside and she did.

Angela started to wonder, "Could he be...?" She had to ask Laura. She didn't have her camera with her at the pool, but she did have her cell phone with a built in camera. Bodine was splashing in the pool in front of her, and she thought about all the times Bodine had taken stealth photographs of her. Sometimes when they traveled abroad, the locals did not like to be photographed without being compensated. Bodine would take a picture of Angela with the focus on the person in the distance. Angela had no practice doing it, but she tried, and was able to get a clear shot of the mystery man.

It was a matter of seconds before she sent the photo to Laura's phone, with the text message, *It can't be Paulo I'm looking at here at the pool, can it?*

Laura called back. "My God it's him. He shaved his head since I saw him last, but there is no mistaking that tattoo. What am I going to do?"

"Hold on, let me go where I can talk," Angela said as she walked to the next pool area. "The wedding is day after tomorrow. You have to tell Jackson. Do you want me and Bo to come over and help figure this out?" Angela could hear Laura breathing hard into the phone. "Hold on Laura, we'll get dressed and be at your place in an hour."

When Angela and Bodine arrived at Laura's condo, Jackson let them in. Angela sat with Laura, to try to calm her, while Jackson paced back and forth.

"All she will say is 'He's in town.'" Jackson said. "Can you guys tell me what is going on?"

"Can you get her a small paper bag to breathe in?" Angela asked. "I'm afraid she's hyperventilating."

After Laura breathed into the bag a few minutes and calmed down, Angela told Jackson what she knew about Paulo Ochoa, and how she had seen him at the pool.

"Why would he come here?" Jackson asked. "He hasn't talked to her in months. What does he want?"

"I think he wants to control me. He doesn't want me to be happy with anybody else," Laura replied. "I'm afraid he might try to hurt me."

Bodine asked, "What do you know about this guy anyway?"

Laura hesitated. She knew her future with Jackson depended on telling all the things that might drive him away. She had kept so much to herself, telling it all would show what a fool she had been.

"Laura, Darling," Jackson began, "we're getting married in two days. I'm going to do everything in my power to protect you, but you have to tell me what we're dealing with."

"At first we just talked on the phone," Laura began. "He was helping me with Portuguese. It was all so innocent and breezy. Then he sent me a plane ticket one-way to Rio. I was shocked. I wondered what kind of man is this to send a ticket to someone he never met. I sent the ticket back, bought my own round-trip ticket, and flew to Rio. We had fun at first. He was spending money left and right, buying me clothes and jewelry, eating out at fabulous restaurants. When I asked what kind of work he did, he said he was taking a vacation to spend the time with me. But every day he had meetings, he said with his family. When I asked too many questions, he got angry and started pushing me around."

Angela said, "So it was before we got to Rio, he had already been hitting you?"

"I'm sorry," Laura said. "I couldn't bring myself to tell it. Not to you and especially not to Jackson."

"So he has money," Jackson said. "Probably dirty money. Wasn't there a drug cartel years ago involving an Ochoa family?"

"I thought they were arrested in Colombia," Bodine said. "Do you think they could be the same people?"

"I sure made a mess of things, didn't I?" Laura began to sob.

"Look, Babe," Jackson said. "We're going to have a wedding, and we're not going to let anybody stop us. We'll just have to make arrangements for bodyguards and whatever other security we need to protect you."

"At such short notice?" Laura asked. "We'll have to postpone the wedding."

"How long have you lived in Las Vegas?" Bodine asked. "You ought to be able to get protection as tight as the Secret Service in Las Vegas. The casinos have such high-tech surveillance, it's like they're protecting Fort Knox."

"Who do you call? I wouldn't think you could find it in the Yellow Pages," Angela said. "But come to think of it, Patti Melt's brother is a pit-boss at Caesars. Maybe he knows someone in security. Is it OK if I call Patti to get her brother's number?"

"Just don't tell Patti what it's about," Laura said. "It's bad enough that the three of you know. Patti would freak out."

"I'll just tell her we want to meet him as long as we're in town anyway." Angela went into the kitchen to make the call.

"How much does Paulo know about the wedding plans?" Jackson asked. "Do you think he knows the reception will be at Caesars, or was it a coincidence he was at the pool?"

"I had the feeling his hooker was checking Angela out for him," Bodine said.

Laura started breathing hard again, and Jackson suggested she go lie down. "Don't worry, Laura, we got this."

Jackson and Bodine started making a plan while Angela was on the phone in the kitchen. They agreed they needed a bodyguard for Laura as soon as they could hire one, to guard her in the condo, in the limo to the church, at the church, and from the church to the reception. They would need additional security at the church and at the reception. Depending on what Paulo did, they might keep the bodyguard until they boarded their plane to New York after the wedding.

"That's going to cost a lot," Bodine said. "Can't some of the guys at the wedding help with protection?"

"You're talking about a bunch of civilians who're coming to Las Vegas for a party," Jackson said. "Would you trust your wife's life to that crowd? After we talk to Patti's brother, maybe we can get a handle on controlling the cost."

"His name is Farrell Melton, and here is his number," Angela said as she came back from the kitchen. "Patti says he's off tomorrow so he can pick her up from the airport. Have you two worked out a plan?"

"We'll see after we talk to Farrell," Jackson said. "Would you check on Laura for me?"

Angela tapped lightly on Laura's bedroom door, and went in. Laura was smoking a cigarette. Angela shook her head. *It's her house, her lungs.* "Does it help to smoke? I thought you were going to pass out just from the anxiety."

"How are we going to get through this? Jackson must hate me," Laura said.

"I don't see him going anywhere. He has a wedding and a honeymoon on his mind. He and Bo are going to talk to Patti's brother, and they will figure it out. Jackson will do everything he can to protect you."

"Thanks, Angela. It's good to hear that coming from you."

Angela gave her a hug, trying not to let on how afraid she was for her friend. The man she saw at the pool looked like someone who could hurt Laura.

* * * *

Jackson left a message on Farrell's voicemail saying he was a friend of Patti's and he needed some help with security in Las Vegas, and to please not mention it to Patti.

Farrell returned the call quickly. "Is Patti OK? What is going on?"

"Patti is fine as far as I know," Jackson replied. "I know she's coming to town tomorrow for my wedding with Laura Murchison."

"Oh yes, QTEE's wedding. How can I help you?"

Jackson gave Farrell a rundown on what was happening with Paulo. "We decided we need to get a bodyguard for Laura until we know she's safe. We don't know anybody in security, and since the reception will be at Caesars, we thought you might know someone."

"I know people who work hotel security, and also a few who work freelance," Farrell said. "I'll make a few calls and see what I can come up with. Let me give you the number for the hotel security. Tell Mr. Potts I told you to call. He can arrange for extra security at the reception."

"Thanks," Jackson said. "I'll call Mr. Potts right away. And don't let on to your sister what trouble we're having."

"I won't say a word to Patti, but she's a Jersey girl. She can handle it."

Jackson called Mr. Potts and explained the need for additional security at the wedding reception.

"I'll assign a man for the reception room," Mr. Potts said. "You'll have to give me a list of names of the invited guests, and a description of Paulo Ochoa. I will need that by tomorrow morning."

Jackson replied, "I can email or FAX you the names today. And we have a photo of Mr. Ochoa."

"Excellent," Mr. Potter said, and he gave Jackson his email address.

"One more thing," Jackson replied. "Will your man be in uniform, or how exactly will he be dressed?"

"All our private guards dress the same as the waiters for your reception, black tuxedo. Nobody will know there is a guard unless you tell it. The guard will ask your guests to give their names so he can check them off on the list. It eliminates party-crashers, and he'll know if Mr. Ochoa shows up."

"That's good," Jackson said. "We don't want our guests to feel like they're under surveillance, or that anybody is in danger. Thanks for your help. I'll get you that list right away."

Jackson called Laura and Angela into the room and told them the plans for the guard at the reception. "I'm waiting for Farrell to call me back about a personal bodyguard for you. Meanwhile, Laura, can you send a list of the invited guests to Mr. Potts at Caesars? Also a photo of Paulo."

Angela could see Bodine was getting antsy. He didn't like being involved in Laura's personal mess. When Angela felt him staring at her to get her attention, she knew he would rather be out at Red Rock Casino.

Angela took her cue and said to Jackson, "You two have this under control and you don't need us anymore, do you?"

"I can handle this from here on. Now we're just waiting for Farrell to call back with information on a bodyguard," Jackson said.

Laura's eyes got bigger with each mention of a guard and a personal bodyguard. "This was going to be a quiet simple wedding and now we need bodyguards. Our friends will think we've gone gangsta on them. I don't like this at all."

"What do you want me to do, Laura?" Jackson asked. "Your safety is important to me. Paulo followed you this far. If you called off the wedding, what would keep him from staying on your trail until he does whatever he has in mind? Besides the guards will be dressed the same as the wait staff. It will look like they're helping out with the reception."

"And a bodyguard for me? What will he look like?"

"He'll be helping the limo driver."

Laura shook her head. She wasn't convinced, but she pulled out her list of names and her laptop to send the email to Mr. Potts.

Bodine stood and pulled Angela up from her seat. "Call us if you need us," he said. "Otherwise, we're heading out." They left as quickly as Bodine could pull Angela away.

The call finally came from Farrell. "Jackson, I have the man for you. He has experience with private security. He's forty, six foot four, weighs about three hundred. He served in the Army during Desert Storm. I have known him personally for several years, and he's the right one for the job.

"I've never met Laura, but I know she has been so nice to my sister and to my nephew when he was in college here. I want the best for the two of you and your marriage. I have a late shift in the casino, but I'm off tomorrow. I can bring him to your place in the morning. I'm supposed to pick Patti up at the airport around noon."

"Thanks, man. That sounds good. What's your man's name?" Jackson asked.

"Taggart Murchison."

"Laura's last name is Murchison. Do you think he might be related?"

"He's right here," Farrell said. "I'll ask him." After a pause, Farrell said, "Tag says he doesn't know Laura."

"Why does the name Taggart Murchison sound familiar?" Jackson asked Laura when he had hung up the phone.

"My ex's name was Taggart. Why do you ask?"

"Farrell is bringing a bodyguard over here tomorrow whose name is Taggart Murchison. He said he doesn't know you."

"There has to be a connection somewhere." Laura said. "That name is too unique for him not to be related to my ex. Did Farrell say how old he is?"

"Forty."

"I married Tag thirty years ago. We stayed married ten years, and he died seven years ago. If he had a son other than Carlton, he never told me," Laura said.

"Well, we'll meet him in the morning. We'll figure it out then."

* * * *

Before Farrell arrived the next morning with the bodyguard, Laura had pulled out old photo albums with pictures of her late ex-husband. She knew she would have to see a resemblance in the young man before she would think of probing further into his background. After the condo guard at the gate called to announce Farrell's arrival, Laura opened her door and waited for them to come out of the elevator. When Tag and Farrell turned to walk down the hall to Laura's unit, she smiled at them. Laura knew the shorter man had to be Farrell. As they came closer, Tag returned the smile, and Laura could see the resemblance.

He has Tag's walk, bounding up on his toes. And that's his smile. Laura had always told Carlton he had half his daddy's smile. His dad had dimples in the corners of his smile. Carlton had only the left dimple, and she could see the bodyguard had the dimple on the right. *And those same eyes, just like when my Tag smiled, his eyes changed from dark brown to blue-black, the corners of his eyes almost squaring off, they were so big. I always told him I could lose myself in those eyes. Plus he's the same pecan-tan with freckles across his nose.*

"My God, you're the image of my late husband, only bigger." Laura said as she brought them into the condo. "My Tag was six feet tall and he never weighed more than a hundred and eighty pounds. Come in. You have to take a look at these photos."

Laura invited Farrell, Jackson, and Taggart to sit around the dining table to look at the photos. They all agreed the resemblance was so striking; the younger Tag had to be related to Laura's late husband.

"I know you came here to talk about a job guarding me," Laura said, "but you'll have to excuse me if I ask some personal questions."

"Ma'am, if you want to know who my father was, I don't know myself. He was never in my life. My mom said he died in Viet Nam," Taggart said.

"Did your mom tell you what his name was?"

"She said I was Taggart Junior."

"I would love to talk to your mom. Do you think it would be too pushy of me to ask her some questions?"

"My mom died of cancer eight years ago," Taggart said.

"I'm so sorry for your loss," Laura said. "And so sorry you didn't find out more about your dad."

By the time Laura, Jackson, and Farrell had finished asking questions, they still didn't know for sure if this man was Laura's stepson. Laura clearly liked him, studying his face, touching his shoulders when she stood behind him looking at photos. She was more at ease than she had been since hearing Paulo was in town.

Farrell had been watching the time to be sure he wouldn't be late picking his sister up from the airport. He decided to summarize the official intent of the meeting by saying, "So we have a good fit? Ms. Laura, are you satisfied with Tag here as your bodyguard?"

"I like him," Laura said.

Farrell had a contract for Laura to sign, agreeing to the cost per day and the requirements for Tag and for Laura. "You can read these over and give me the signed copies tomorrow," Farrell said. "I'll call Potts and tell him to expect the papers tomorrow."

"Will Tag stay here in my condo tonight?" Laura asked.

"It's stated in the contract he will stay with you until you leave Las Vegas, or you are satisfied that Paulo is no longer a threat."

Jackson interjected, "He can stay in the guest room. I'll be here tonight, too. I have a reservation at Caesars tomorrow night, before the wedding, and then we have the Bridal Suite after the wedding. I surely hope we can dispose of Paulo before our wedding night."

"Let me tell you a little about my style, Mr. Jackson, Ms. Laura," Tag began. "You will know I'm here, but after a while I'll be like a large piece of furniture. You don't have to include me in your conversations. I'll make my own meals while I'm here, and clean up after myself. I will be awake before dawn, and I won't sleep until you are in for the night. I will make periodic sweeps of the condo, including outside areas during all the hours you are here. Your scheduled activities include a bachelor party tomorrow night. Ms. Laura may have ladies here tomorrow. I have the names on the list."

"I don't know how to ask you this, Tag," Laura said. "How should I introduce you to my son, Carlton? I want you two to know each other, but at the same time, I don't want to distract you from the job we brought you here for. I'm not even sure I want anybody to know you are a bodyguard. My friends Angela and Bodine already know the plan, and they will keep quiet about it. And Farrell will, too."

"We can wait until after the reception," Tag said. "Carlton's focus should be on his family and friends. I'll be the large piece of furniture by the door. After a while everybody will forget I'm there, and you can enjoy your party as you planned it."

Laura breathed a sigh of relief, "You have eased my mind. There will be plenty of time after the reception for Carlton to get to know you."

After Farrell left, Tag took his small bag into the guest room, and quietly returned to the kitchen where he could watch Laura and Jackson in the living room watching television. He felt a real connection to Laura, and told himself he might have to fight Paulo to protect her.

CHAPTER SIXTEEN

The Wedding

The wedding party consisted of bride, groom, best man, matron of honor, and Laura's son, Carlton to give her away. Laura didn't want to waste time with a wedding rehearsal. It would be a small gathering, and the minister would tell them where to go and what to say, anyway. No lighting candles, no mingling sand, just two rings. There was no bridal shower; the new couple had two households of furnishings to merge. Carlton insisted on having a bachelor party. A few internet friends were invited to the wedding, and Carlton contacted the men to plan to hang out the night before the wedding. Jackson moved into the hotel the day before the wedding, leaving Laura at the condo to prepare for the big day. Angela was there at Laura's house to make sure she didn't get cold feet.

Angela noticed the big guy trying to be unobtrusive, sitting at Laura's desk. "The bodyguard, huh? Are you comfortable with him here?"

"Jackson and I interviewed him extensively, and we're both cool with it. He makes me feel safe. He told us to act like he's not there, and it will be easier to go on with our plans."

"I am so glad it worked out," Angela said. "If Paulo does show up, that refrigerator can handle him with one hand tied behind his back. I'm so happy you're going on with the wedding."

"It's amazing how we got to this day. God must be smiling on us. Jackson has the honeymoon all planned. We'll fly to New York the day after the wedding and spend the night at the Marriott Marquis right there on Broadway. He's like Bodine, he's not crazy about New York, but he knows I am. We'll see whatever show we can get tickets for."

"And you're going to Paris." Angela squealed as if she were the one about to make the trip. "Make sure you have your walking shoes. There is so much to see."

"After two days in New York, we have an overnight flight to Paris," Laura said. "I think Jackson had a travel agent to do the hotel reservations in Paris. Five nights in Paris, and finally back home to Memphis."

"How do you like Memphis? I've spent a couple of days there myself. We hung out on Beale Street and went to B.B. King's, but I didn't get any feel for what it's like to live there."

"Memphis doesn't have the same spark for me as New York or Las Vegas," Laura said.

"Or Paris?"

"But we've been happy. I guess after all we've been through. And you know, Angela, I really prayed for that man. I asked God to make this right, don't let me screw it up again."

"You really love him, don't you?" Angela asked.

"Yeah. Now where is our bachelorette party? I guess it's nobody but you and me, and Patti arrived yesterday. She's spending some time with her brother. I'll give her a call and ask her to come over."

"Well let's get this party humping," Angela said.

"What do you know about humping?"

"I just thought it sounded good."

* * * *

The morning of the wedding, Angela dressed in her bridesmaid's gown, a V-neck teal chiffon dress with charmeuse empire band and slightly shirred A-line skirt, accented with sequins that sparkled as she walked. Bodine drove her to Laura's condo and left her at the door. Only the bridesmaid would see the bride before the wedding. The ever-vigilant bodyguard stayed out of the way.

Laura met Angela at the door in her bathrobe. "I don't want to put the dress on until right before the limo gets here. Why don't you hang up your dress and I can get you a robe to wear. We want to be fresh as daisies for this god-awful hot day. Who made me have a wedding in August?"

"Don't look at me," Angela said. "By the way, I didn't ask you who is coming."

"There are five of us in the wedding party. And Keisha and Jamal. Jackson's son and daughter-in-law. Then Patti, Dillon and his wife, Harman and a friend, Lester...I told him he could bring a date...not Bonita, Winmyheart and her latest man, Lil-Miss is coming from San Juan with her husband."

Angela said, "I can never keep up with where she is after she didn't go back to New Orleans."

"That's twenty total. And I didn't tell you who is officiating."

"Who?"

"Sistah Pastah. She makes lucky twenty-one."

"Oh my. You know I have never met her in person. I think she was the one who got me involved in an AIDS ministry at my church. Her life is quite a testimony. You talked to her a lot, didn't you, when she was deciding to go from helping HIV victims at the church to going to seminary and getting ordained. Your marriage will be blessed. But do you think she will approve of being the winning Black Jack card?"

When the condo guard called to notify Laura the limo had arrived, she put on her wedding dress with Angela's help to button the thirty pearl buttons up the back. When Angela stepped back to admire her friend as a bride, she had to catch her breath.

Laura asked, "Are you OK?"

"Oh my goodness yes. It's your dress, it's like I dreamed it, with the buttons and all the lace and the cut-out shoulders. You did say the wedding would be at a church, right? Not one of those 24-hour chapels."

"It's a small church, Truth Chapel Baptist Church. How do you like that? A chapel church."

* * * *

The limo ride was as Angela had dreamed it, except they arrived at a small church instead of a chintzy all-night chapel. She had not dreamed there would be a bodyguard, but he sat in the front with the driver, and was the first to step out of the limo. He told the ladies to wait until he inspected the church. He told the pastor, Rev. Goodwin, he wanted to make sure all doors were locked to prevent party crashers and paparazzi from getting into the wedding. The pastor's eyes grew big at the idea of having a celebrity in his little church. He greeted Laura when she climbed out of the limo. "Ms. Murchison, you make a lovely bride. I'm so happy you chose our church for your special day. Your lady pastor is already here. I told her I would send you to the office when you arrived."

Laura thanked Rev. Goodwin and followed him to his office. Tag followed at a distance and took his post outside the pastor's office. Angela went into the fellowship hall to make sure the rest of the wedding party was in place. Carlton introduced himself along with his wife, Keisha and little Jamal. Jamal wore a little tuxedo to match the men in the wedding, down to his little boutonnière and patent leather shoes. Bodine was there helping Jackson with his boutonnière. Angela gave them both a hug and went to check to see if the preparations in the sanctuary were as Laura had requested. The flowers were in place on the altar, and the white carpet had been placed for the couple to kneel for their wedding prayer and blessing. The organist had already started to play background music. When she noticed Angela checking on things, she stopped playing and went to talk to her.

"Miss, are you the wedding planner?"

Angela said, "I'm the matron of honor, but the bride did ask me to check on things."

"I'm Odessa Goodwin, the pastor's wife. My husband said I should play some background music, the processional for the ring bearer and matron of honor, the bridal march, and recessional. Is that all the music she wants?"

"That's it exactly."

"She doesn't have anyone to sing?" Mrs. Goodwin asked.

"No, ma'am. She wants a simple wedding."

"I could sing 'Oh Promise Me.' Everyone loves to hear me sing that one. There's never a dry eye in the house when I sing."

Angela remembered the last time she heard "Oh Promise Me" at a wedding. It must have been forty years ago, and the soloist sounded like a chicken squawking.

"Oh I'm sure you do have a lovely voice, Mrs. Goodwin, but the bride was very specific. She wants a very simple and short wedding."

Angela went to check on Laura, and felt her heart soar when she met Sistah Pastah. It was her screen name on BK, and the only name Angela knew. She looked exactly like her photos, but Angela never knew what a petite woman she was. She was dressed in a white ministerial robe making her look angelic. When Angela heard her voice, she remembered the online conversations when she pretended to sing to Laura...*OOOOH OOOOH. You don't know my name.*

This is just perfect, Angela thought. She felt Sistah Pastah's protective presence already, and said a silent prayer asking God to protect Laura and Jackson from all evil, and to bless their marriage.

* * * *

Some people wouldn't think of having children in their wedding; others couldn't imagine a wedding without them. Laura's grandson, Jamal was two years old, and had no idea what the occasion was all about. All he knew was he had a tuxedo like his Daddy's and a yellow rose pinned to his lapel. His mama said he needed a rehearsal; Laura said he would be fine.

"The whole ceremony will only last fifteen minutes," Laura had said, "unless Sistah Pastah gets religion and wants to give a homily or something. Let the baby do his thing."

While Laura was in an office somewhere preparing to enter the small sanctuary, Jamal was on the back seat with his mama, playing with the pillow with a large faux ring tied in the middle. He tried biting the ring off, pulling it off, but it stayed put. It was nice for chewing, though. The cold metal felt good on his sore gums. Then he put the pillow on his head and turned his head quickly left and right to see if it would stay on. He found if he turned his head really fast, he could propel the pillow into the center aisle. Keisha decided to do as her mother-in-law had instructed and "Let the baby do his thing." The pillow flew into the aisle and Jamal went to retrieve it, three or four times. Next, he started on the yellow ribbon tassels hanging on each corner of the pillow. He had zipped the pillow into the aisle when the music started and the congregation stood up. People in the audience were taking pictures. Jamal pulled the pillow out of the way barely in time. Laura and Carlton were standing in the doorway at the back of the church, telling Jamal to go with the pillow. He was supposed to go first down the aisle when the organist played the ring bearer's music, but Jamal was standing his ground. He didn't want to get in trouble.

Laura gave Angela a wink to go ahead down the aisle, and then gave a signal to Mrs. Goodwin to start the bride's processional music, "Here Comes the Bride." Laura gave Jamal a smile and a wink as she passed him on her procession to the altar. Carlton gave him the look. Carlton's evil eye meant Jamal had better sit down or he would be in trouble.

Keisha decided she would get Jamal up front one way or another. Once Laura reached the front of the church, Keisha told Jamal to take the pillow to Grandma. Jamal was happy to comply, he had been still as long as he could. He grabbed the pillow and ran faster than any of the amateur photographers could react, up to the front, handed the pillow to Laura, and flew fast as the wind, back to his seat in the back with Keisha. All the wedding guests laughed and applauded the little ring bearer, who was sure he had done a good thing.

Angela stood beside Laura, Bodine beside Jackson. Angela's eyes stayed fixed on the bodyguard who stood beside the organ. *If he so much as flinches, I'll know something is going down.* She was so distracted Laura had to poke her to take the bridal bouquet.

Laura and Jackson had requested a traditional service since they had not prepared their own vows. Sistah Pastah opened with, "Dearly Beloved," and Angela sighed and thought, we're going to get through this. When Sistah said, "if anyone can show just reason why these two should not be united as husband and wife, let them speak now or forever keep their peace," Angela could see the bodyguard's eyes fixed on the back door, so she turned to look at the door, and within seconds, Laura turned, Jackson turned, Bodine turned, all looking at the rear door. Then Lester sitting in the second pew turned, and before the Sistah could continue with the "I require and charge you both," everyone, including Mrs. Goodwin was looking at the back door.

When nobody entered the church, Lester turned back to the front and gave Angela a questioning shrug with palms turned up and mouthed, *What?* Angela gave him an innocent smile as if nothing had happened. The vows continued without another distraction. Sistah Pastah said the benediction and after Jackson grabbed Laura in a dip for a kiss, Sistah introduced the couple as Mr. and Mrs. Jackson Gooding.

After the ceremony, the bodyguard checked the exterior of the church before he allowed Laura and Jackson to take the waiting limousine to Caesars Palace Hotel and Casino where they proceeded to the bridal suite. A large van took the rest of the party to Caesars where the security guards dressed as waiters, escorted them to a private dining room for the reception. Before the guests could enter the reception, the large muscular waiter standing by the door asked for their names to check off the guest list. Three dining tables were arranged in a U shape with place cards identifying the seating as desired by the bride. An adjoining room had an open bar and a DJ who played smooth jazz and R&B oldies. Angela urged the guests to get on their feet and mingle in the bar room. Two waiters circulated through the room with trays of hors d'oeuvres and champagne. The trays containing shellfish were labeled with large yellow smiley faces saying "SHELLFISH" in big bold letters.

Sistah Pastah asked Angela, "Is that an inside joke or something?"

Angela laughed. "Something like that. Jackson had a run-in with some shrimp a few months ago. It put him in the hospital."

Lester was there with a date. They spent a lot of time on the dance floor doing some Mambo-Salsa something before he introduced her. "Hey everybody, this is Nabila. Nabila this is everybody."

The whole room said, "Hi Nabila" and went back to what they were doing. The other people from BK, Dillon, Patti, Winmyheart, and Lil-Miss, were huddled together reminiscing about the old days on BK. When Laura and Jackson made their entrance, the DJ played Luther Vandross' "Here and Now," for their first dance.

Laura had shed the veil and the removable train from her dress and traded her spiked heels for bejeweled sneakers. After the waiters seated everyone in the dining room, the headwaiter explained the menu. They had a choice of filet mignon, chicken Kiev, or a vegetarian dish. The waiters took their orders and brought wine.

Before the wait staff could serve the main course, Tag moved quickly from his corner behind Laura to the door where Angela heard loud voices outside the room. Tag recognized and grabbed Paulo who wore a tuxedo and carried a large wrapped present the size of a breadbox. With Paulo was the young lady from the pool, wearing a long silver sequined gown. The reception guests became quiet as they tried to listen to the conversation outside the door.

"No, I was not invited. I just want to give this present to Laura and wish for her a happy marriage," Paulo said.

Tag grabbed the box and handed it over to a member of hotel security who took it outside.

"I mean no harm to anyone," Paulo said. "Just let me speak to Laura, and I will be on my way."

Tag held Paulo back and frisked him. After another member of hotel security took Paulo's date away to be questioned, Laura appeared at the door with Jackson by her side.

"I just wanted to see you, how beautiful you are," Paulo said. "And I wanted to see the man who won your heart when I could not. Please forgive me for hurting you and causing you to fear me. You will always be my special lady." Then he knelt, and kissed Laura's hand.

Laura shivered and started gasping for breath. Jackson guided her to a chair. "She's had too much excitement this week," he said. "Can someone get me a paper bag?"

One of the waiters provided a paper bag for Laura to breathe into until her breathing returned to normal. Tag had taken Paulo to the security offices where Mr. Potts' staff detained him for questioning. Tag returned to the reception and told Laura, "They will keep Paulo and his date for a few hours, and then take them to the Las Vegas Metropolitan Police Department. I expect the police will charge Paulo with stalking. They may even have him deported."

"When I saw him, at first I was frightened," Laura said. "But after he kissed my hand, I thought what a sweet boy he still is under the surface. I hope they won't rough him up too much."

Jackson gave her a hug, "You shouldn't have such a soft heart for that guy. Let's forget him and get on with dinner."

"Before we do that, I need to introduce Tag to Carlton," Laura said.

Carlton had been watching during the scuffle with Paulo, but had stayed at Keisha's side shielding Jamal. After Paulo had been taken away, he stepped forward, waiting for Laura to explain what was going on.

"Mom, who was that man?" Carlton asked.

"I'll have to tell you the whole long story when we can do it in private," Laura said. "But now I want you to meet Tag." She motioned for Tag to come to join them. "I met this gentleman only two days ago to hire him as a bodyguard."

"A bodyguard, Mom? Why?"

"Baby, that's all part of the long story. But the good part is who this gentleman is. His name is Taggart Murchison."

"That's Dad's name. What? Who is this?"

"Just look at him," Laura said. "I know your dad wasn't around for most of your life, but you have pictures of him. Doesn't he look like your dad?"

"Mom, are you saying this man is my brother?"

Tag extended his hand for Carlton to shake. Carlton stared in disbelief for a few seconds. Then when he could see the resemblance, the eyes, and the same dimple he had himself, Carlton took Tag's hand, and grabbed him in an embrace. Then the two men stepped back, looked at each other, and laughed until their eyes brimmed over with tears.

"Mom, how did this happen? Did you ever know about Tag?" Carlton asked.

"Baby, I don't think your dad even knew about Tag," Laura said. "But when I heard his name, and saw him, I knew he had to be your brother. His Mom told him his dad died in Viet Nam, and she died before she could tell him the truth. I don't know how Tag feels about having a brother, but I hope you two can be friends. It would sure make me feel better about moving to Memphis leaving you here without me, knowing you have a bodyguard in the family."

Carlton shook his head. "Mom, you didn't worry about me

when you went off without telling me where you were going."

"That was different," Laura said while she tried to hide her guilty eyes.

By this time, the servers had begun bringing dinner plates. Jackson stepped forward and asked, "Can we eat now?"

The wedding guests had witnessed the introduction of Taggart Murchison and were chatting amongst themselves about the happy events of the day when Mr. Potts appeared at the door carrying a large shopping bag. He approached Laura and Jackson with his bill for security services, but he needed to give them an update on the status of Paulo Ochoa. He tried to speak as quietly as possible so the guests would not hear, but the whispering had the opposite effect. The room became quiet.

"I wanted you to have this gift from Mr. Ochoa. The bomb squad dunked it in the closest pool and found it to be an actual gift. Fortunately, it did withstand the water." Mr. Potts handed the shopping bag to Laura, who smiled as she took out Paulo's gift, a large crystal vase.

Potts continued, "We turned Mr. Ochoa over to the police who will detain him until you are safely away on your honeymoon."

Lester, "TheGuy" stood and applauded. The other guests followed Lester's lead and filled the room with applause and laughter.

"Laura, please, can we eat now?" Lester begged holding his hands together.

All the guests were served, and they did eat. Laura was too

excited to eat and took Jackson with her to mingle with the guests at their tables. When the guests had finished the main course, a server wheeled in a table with the wedding cake. Laura and Jackson did the corny cake-cutting ritual of feeding each other, and the waitress sliced and served the remainder of the cake. Everyone continued dancing, the men taking turns dancing with Laura, while Jackson mingled with the ladies until the waiter brought the bill for the reception to Laura and Jackson. The couple did their last circulation through the group, thanking everyone for coming. When Angela asked if there was anything else she needed, Laura assured her the celebration had been as perfect as it could be in spite of Paulo. Angela helped the others to leave the private room and suggested they might like to gamble.

Angela was exhausted. She knew Bodine liked to gamble, especially when he was wearing a tuxedo. He said it brought him luck. It made him feel like James Bond, sitting at a roulette table while drinking champagne. She kissed him goodnight and went up to their room where she dropped her dress and shoes on the floor and fell into bed. She didn't hear Bodine come in at ten. He was still wide awake. He had made a big hit on a dollar slot machine, and he was still feeling all the champagne from the wedding, and from the casino.

"Angela, are you sleep?"

Angela opened one eye and looked at him. "Huh?"

"This is our last night in Vegas, and we didn't go to the fountains. Put your dress back on, and let's go hear a couple of songs at the Fountains of Bellagio. They stop playing at midnight."

Angela knew they had their tradition. The teal chiffon lay in a heap on the floor, but it didn't look too bad when she put it on. She wished she had Laura's bridal sneakers to wear instead of the dyed-to-match satin shoes. Bodine pulled out her flip-flops. "Nobody will notice."

Angela splashed some water on her face, combed her hair, and swished some mouthwash. "OK, let's do it."

At night, the fountains played every fifteen minutes on the quarter hour. Bodine's favorites were the show tunes with a gambling theme, "Hey Big Spender" and "Luck Be a Lady Tonight." Angela liked "Time to Say Goodbye" and the theme from *Titanic*. They stood until they each heard at least one favorite song with a big splash from the fountains timed to coincide with the musical crescendo. It was getting close to midnight when they walked back down the street to Caesars and to bed.

* * * *

Angela's cell phone woke them early the next morning. They had a ten a.m. flight home, and had to check out of the hotel and return the rental car in time to be at the airport by eight. The wait for the security check was long with lines snaking left and right between ropes. Angela dreaded going through security on any trip, more so since Bodine had a hip replacement a few years ago. He set off the metal detector, so Angela would have to gather up her things and his...jacket, shoes, belt, laptop, and carry the whole collection to a bench where she could put her shoes and clothes back on while Bodine got the personal pat-down.

After completing the security check, they bought breakfast and found a place to sit and have their sausage biscuit and tea. A voice called out from behind, "Angela and Bodine." It was Laura with Jackson in tow on their way to board their flight to New York.

Angela couldn't stop herself from asking, "Did you sleep well last night?" After a chuckle, she continued. "All kidding aside, it was a beautiful wedding. And it was so good to have your favorite peeps from BK. I know Facebook will be buzzing with comments when everybody gets back online."

"Did you get a lot of pictures?" Laura asked. "We decided not to hire a photographer. All the posing would have been such a waste of time, time away from our friends we haven't talked to in so long."

Angela said, "You know they will be posting photos on Facebook. I hope you all have a camera to take pictures of Paris."

"I have my camera," Jackson said. "I can't wait to be with Laura in Paris. We might email you some photos of us."

Bodine said, "Be sure to take her to the Moulin Rouge."

When the loudspeaker announced the flight to Raleigh boarding at gate D23, Angela said, "They're boarding our flight. We need to get going."

They had hugs all around and Angela and Laura started to tear up. They said goodbye and off they went.

"I hope there aren't any more people you need to marry off," Bodine said.

"We still have Stephen," Angela said. "He has an online sweetie in California."

"I hope they move to the same zip code before they think about getting married. Does she even know he's in a wheelchair?"

Angela rolled her eyes at Bodine and laughed as they hurried off to their gate.

CHAPTER SEVENTEEN

The Aftermath

The Beaudoins arrived home before dark, exhausted, but not too tired to upload their photos of the wedding. Bodine wanted to be the first to post his on Facebook. The wedding wasn't a secret anymore, and all the detractors could say what they wanted.

After Bodine posted the photos, there were OOHs and AHHs comments from their friends. They had to admit Jackson was as handsome as Laura was beautiful. In addition, people posted comments saying how happy they looked. Apparently, no other wedding guests had arrived home yet, so Bodine went to bed happy he had gotten the scoop on everybody else, although he only had photos of the reception. He knew Lester had taken photos at the wedding.

By morning, the photo elves had been working overtime, and all the guests from the wedding had wedding pictures on their Facebook walls. Angela did receive an email from Laura:

Mother Confessor,

I am so blessed to have a friend like you to stick by me through all my foolishness and help me see what I couldn't, right in front of my eyes. Thank you for being our own personal matchmaker.

Please thank all the guests for being there for us. And email me one of the photos Bodine took at the reception. Pick out the one you think makes me look the most gorgeous. ;)

Luv you,

A1QTEE

Angela chose a photo from the reception of Laura and Jackson dancing, looking into each other's eyes. They looked so much in love.

Bodine had to pick up Dusty from doggy day care. They had trimmed his hair, and somehow "locked" it so he had a fresh new mop head look.

The rest of the day, they spent resting, recovering from the wedding festivities and all the food and champagne. They called their sons to tell them of the fabulous wedding in Las Vegas. Aaron made some polite remarks but mostly said, "uh, huh." He had had his own wedding experience. It seemed his wedding lasted longer than the marriage. Stephen made some comments about when he gets married, making Angela raise her eyebrows. Nevertheless, she resisted making any comment about his Facebook sweetie, even though he probably knew she had read his Facebook changes in relationship status. Nathan asked a lot of questions about the church in Las Vegas, and the venue for the reception. After those phone calls, Angela asked Bodine if Nathan had said anything about getting married again. Bodine said, "I'm staying out of it."

Two days later, Wednesday

Angela woke up at five in the morning, wide awake the way she often did after getting back from a vacation. Even though they were still working on dirty laundry and a stack of unread mail, Angela decided it was a good time to catch up on her reading. She had taken her Kindle with her to Las Vegas, but the only reading she had done was around the pool before the wedding. She had two book clubs plus an online discussion group to keep up with, and she had read only half of one of the three books for the month.

She went to the kitchen to make breakfast and found Dusty peeping up at her from his crate. It was too early for him to go for a walk and he settled down to watch Angela make a cup of tea and her usual bowl of oatmeal. Angela turned on the TV, with the volume just loud enough for background noise. The early morning news was on, and the morning anchor interrupted her usual local news saying, "We have a newsflash from the AP News wire." She continued with the breaking news.

Air France officials have reported that a plane has disappeared between New York City and Paris with 228 people on board this morning. The officials believe the Airbus A330-200 aircraft crashed after running into lightning and thunderstorms over the Atlantic Ocean. Early reports from Air France officials say that there were 58 US Citizens on board. We will bring you more information as this story develops.

Angela's ears perked up at the word "disappeared." She wasn't sure what she had heard as she turned up the volume, and stood staring at the TV mounted on the wall in the kitchen. "No, it couldn't be. No."

The whistle on the kettle screamed, shaking Angela out of her stupor. She turned off the burner and continued to stare at the TV screen, thinking she could will it to give out more information.

Fifteen minutes later, the news anchor repeated the same information, this time adding the flight number. *Flight 842Z from New York's JFK Airport to Charles de Gaulle Airport Paris has disappeared.*

Angela didn't know Laura's flight number, or even which airline, but how many flights could there have been from JFK to Paris last night? She was trembling too much to pour the hot water over her teabag. Then the tears came freely, down her cheeks and onto her bathrobe.

The time slipped away while Angela stood in the kitchen watching the screen. When the six o'clock news began, the lead story was 216 passengers and twelve crew members were believed killed in a crash of an Air France plane over the North Atlantic. If no survivors were found, it would be the worst loss of life involving an Air France plane in the firm's 75-year history.

Angela sat frozen with a cold cup of tea and a bowl of cold oatmeal. "What do I do now?" she asked the TV screen.

Bodine answered from the doorway, "I heard. Have they said anything about the passengers?"

Angela shook her head.

Bodine said, "Why don't you go put some clothes on. I'll take Dusty out, and then we'll see about some hot breakfast for you when I get back."

Angela went upstairs and walked into the stall shower with her robe on. She stood under the showerhead crying until she couldn't cry anymore. She dressed and went back downstairs. By ten a.m. the airline had a list of passenger names that they would make public after contacting next of kin.

"What do I do now?" she asked.

"Let's take Dusty for another walk," Bodine said. "We need to get away from the TV."

The rest of the day slogged by, and Angela moved through the mud of the day, walking in circles and listening for more news. They didn't dare go on Facebook. Nobody else knew Laura's travel plans. Even if they heard the news of the plane crash, they wouldn't associate it with Laura.

When Angela thought she couldn't endure waiting another minute, the phone rang—a call from Las Vegas.

"Ms. Angela, it's me Carlton. I just got a call from Air France. Mama was on that plane."

Wednesday Morning, the Plaza Hotel, Manhattan

Daylight was just beginning to peek through the heavy curtains, when Laura opened her eyes. She leaned over, supporting herself on one elbow, and watched Jackson sleeping. She didn't want to wake him, but just in case he was almost awake, she whispered, "PSST."

Jackson opened one eye and smiled at her. "Good morning, Mrs. Gooding," he said as he kissed her. "You made us miss our flight."

Laura giggled and said, "No, you made us miss our flight."

They continued back and forth, both laughing, each blaming the other, until they resumed their lovemaking from the night before. When they were spent, Laura got up and took in their hotel room. They had been too sleepy when they checked in late last night, to notice how shabby the room was. Now Laura noticed the scratched furniture, the worn upholstery, and the dusty drapes. She went into the bathroom, and winced.

"Jackson, I haven't seen fixtures this old since 1970," she called from the bathroom. "I'm not complaining, mind you. I'm thankful your agent could get us a hotel in Manhattan at short notice last night."

"She did say the Plaza is being renovated, and we might be in one of the last rooms to be completed. We can handle it for a few days while she gets us another flight and changes our reservation in Paris, can't we?" Jackson responded.

"Sure, Baby, no problem."

When Laura had finished in the bathroom, she opened the drapes to look out on the view.

"Jackson, you have to see this," Laura said. "We have the best view. We're looking down on Central Park."

"That's nice." Jackson tried to be polite.

"I know you're not crazy about New York, but we have to go for a walk before it gets hot. Come on, let's get dressed."

"Our travel agent is supposed to call us when she's made arrangements for us," he said.

"You have your phone. We don't have to sit around here waiting for her call."

Laura was so excited about another day in the city, she dragged Jackson as far as their feet would take them through Central Park, where they watched mommies push their baby strollers and perambulators, joggers getting their daily endorphins, dogs walking their owners, birders following the latest app on their iPhones for a sighting of another feathered creature to check off on their lists. They bought coffee and fresh buns, hot dogs from street vendors, and bottled water to get them through the morning until Jackson started to droop.

"OK, I guess we've walked enough," Laura said as they stopped to rest on a park bench.

"Why don't we get a taxi to a nice restaurant for lunch, and just chill for a while," Jackson said.

"I know just the place," Laura said. "*B. Smith's*. It's not far."

"Where do we get a taxi?" Jackson asked.

"My dear, just follow me," Laura said as she took Jackson by the hand and led him to the nearest street corner. When Laura stepped out from the curb, Jackson grabbed her around the waist to protect her from the oncoming traffic.

"Let me handle this," Laura said as she stepped out into the traffic as a taxi approached, and raised her hand for one to stop.

"They will always stop for a pretty lady, won't they," Jackson said. Laura gave him a wink as they climbed into the taxi. When they arrived at *B. Smith's*, Jackson was so relieved to be inside in the air-conditioning, it didn't matter when they had to wait for thirty minutes to be seated. After they had B's appetizer sampler, they couldn't finish the soup and salad they had ordered.

Jackson said, "This place is a little too girly for me, but I don't mind having a bit of a rest."

"Are you too tired to go to see some museums?" Laura asked.

"Why don't we go back to the hotel for a little nap first," Jackson said.

It was all Jackson could do to keep his eyes open in the taxi ride back to the Plaza. When they arrived, Jackson remembered they had not heard anything from their travel agent.

"Maybe I need to call her," he said as he pulled his phone out of his pocket. When he saw that it was off he said, "I guess it would help if I had left it on." When he powered his phone on, it started to beep with text messages. He gave Laura a helpless look and handed her his phone. "I don't know how to do text messages."

Laura shook her head and grinned at him as she read the

incoming display. "You have three messages from Sally." Then she read them, "Call me…Call me immediately…This is urgent." And there was a voice mail message from Sally, "Jackson, I hope you have your phone with you. I need to talk to you right away."

Jackson took the phone and called Sally, their travel agent. "Hi Sally, I guess I had my phone off all day. What's up?"

"I was getting really worried," Sally said. "I even called the front desk at your hotel, and they said you didn't answer. Haven't you guys turned on the news at all today?"

"No, it *is* our honeymoon, you know. What's on the news?" Jackson asked.

"Your flight to Paris crashed last night over the Atlantic," Sally said. "They reported 228 people died."

Jackson stood stone-faced as he turned to look at Laura, not knowing what to say, but he repeated what Sally had told him, "Our flight to Paris crashed last night." Then he dropped the phone and grabbed Laura in his arms. "All those people died, and we're still here." They both started to cry. "God saved us," he said.

Jackson remembered Sally was on the line and picked his phone up. "Sally, are you still there?"

"I'm here. Now you need to tell me what to do about Paris."

"Give me and Laura some time to think about it, and I'll call you back," he said.

"One more thing," Sally said. "I told a friend here in Memphis about what happened, your missing the plane and all. He's a newscaster on the local news, and he wants to interview you and

Laura. Think about that, too, and let me know. They can do it from the studio in New York."

"OK Sally, I'll get back to you."

"What is it we need to think about?" Laura asked when Jackson had hung up.

"What to do about Paris, and do we want to be interviewed?"

"First I'm thinking about Carlton. He must have heard the news. I need to call him and you need to call your son."

They both reached for their phones. Jackson went into the bathroom so they could each hear.

"Baby it's me! We missed our flight. We're in New York and we're safe," Laura said, when she made the call. She could hear Carlton gasp on the other end.

"Mama, I love you so much," Carlton said. "It's a miracle you weren't on that plane. You and Jackson need to come on back to Vegas so I can hug you."

ABOUT THE AUTHOR

Sarah Gordon Weathersby is the youngest of seven siblings, and the first to migrate back to the South after living in DC, New Jersey and New York. She is a retired Information Technology professional. She lives in Raleigh with her husband, and imaginary dog, Dusty.

Sarah is the author of a memoir, *Motherless Child - stories from a life*, and publisher of a family saga, *The Gordons of Tallahassee*, written by her sister LaVerne Gordon Goodridge.

Tell Them I Died is her first work of fiction.

You can contact her online at www.sarahweathersby.com

http://blogspot.sarahweathersby.com

http://www.facebook.com/saraphen

And Twitter @saraphen